# The Deflowered Garden

# The Deflowered Garden

Tanya South

Elm Hill

A Division of
HarperCollins Christian Publishing

www.elmhillbooks.com

## The Deflowered Garden



Published in Nashville, Tennessee, by Elm Hill, an imprint of Thomas Nelson. Elm Hill and Thomas Nelson are registered trademarks of HarperCollins Christian Publishing, Inc.

Elm Hill titles may be purchased in bulk for educational, business, fund-raising, or sales promotional use. For information, please e-mail SpecialMarkets@ThomasNelson.com.

Publisher's Note: This novel is a work of fiction. Names, characters, places, and incidents are either products of the author's imagination or used fictitiously. All characters are fictional, and any similarity to people living or dead is purely coincidental.



**Library of Congress Cataloging-in-Publication Data**

Library of Congress Control Number: 2018963709

ISBN 978-0-310103554 (Paperback)
ISBN 978-0-310103851 (Hardbound)
ISBN 978-0-310103691 (eBook)

DEDICATED TO THE LOST SHEEP

*Matthew 18:12–13, NIV*

*"What do you think? If a man owns a hundred sheep, and one of them wanders away, will he not leave the ninety-nine on the hills and go to look for the one that wandered off? And if he finds it, truly I tell you, he is happier about that one sheep than about the ninety-nine that did not wander off.*

# Table of Contents

# Prologue

## The Beauty in the Garden

De-flow-er: [dih-**flou**-er]: to steal or violently remove beauty, freshness, sanctity, or purity.

Genesis 1:31 – God saw all that he had made, and it was very good.

As my paintbrush carefully touched the beautiful white canvas, my imagination was running wild. I saw an intriguing, astonishing garden coming to life. The gardener meticulously designed every intricate detail of it; from cultivating the rich, fertilized soil, to planting and sowing each seed. Every flower had been planted with careful thought. The gardener then watered and nurtured what he had planted. As a result of his gardening and watching over the garden, it reaped its lovely flowers. The garden stimulated my senses. I could see the beauty, I could touch and feel the texture of each flower, and I could smell the sweet, distinct fragrances of each one. I could even taste the succulent nectar of a particular flower. I saw what this garden produced. It's beautiful, the blossomed and even the budding flowers. The unique, sacred, and lovely quality that each one held was most fascinating to me. The array of alluring colors was sparkling from each distinct blooming flower, while resting on a deep-green bed of grass. Humanity is also that of a delightful garden. Each human being, each woman, each man, is the unique flower that first started out as a seed. Our Heavenly Father, God, is the gardener and creator, who made each of us uniquely magnificent in our own way. But like weeds, the devil takes what is purely beautiful and attempts to pervert it. His mission is to kill, steal, and destroy the purity in the garden. He tried to destroy it with his lies and deception. He attempted to taint the image of what was fearfully and wonderfully made; he twisted the truth and turned it into shame. He *deflowered* the garden; he *deflowered* Adam and Eve. When Eve believed the lie that the devil whispered to her and then baited Adam in, sin entered into the garden, into the world. I believed that lie, too, for many years, living in shame, living with the evil that had been done to me in secret. For a long time, I didn't believe that I was good enough. But God sees otherwise. When he created us, he knew his creation was very good. In the Bible, it says in John 8:12: "When Jesus spoke again to the people, he said, 'I am the light of the world. Whoever follows me will never walk in darkness, but will have the light of life.'" What's in darkness will always be exposed with the light. What the devil used to harm you, shame you, break you shall be exposed to the truth, and the truth shall set you free! The truth that because of what Jesus did on the cross, we are forgiven, redeemed, and worthy.

## CHAPTER ONE

# INTERRUPTED GARDEN

GENESIS 3:1–7

Now the serpent was more crafty than any of the wild animals the Lord God had made. He said to the woman, "Did God really say, 'You must not eat from any tree in the garden'?" The woman said to the serpent, "We may eat fruit from the trees in the garden, but God did say, 'You must not eat fruit from the tree that is in the middle of the garden, and you must not touch it, or you will die. You will not certainly die," the serpent said to the woman, For God knows that when you eat from it your eyes will be opened, and you will be like God, knowing good and evil." When the woman saw that the fruit of the tree was good for food and pleasing to the eye, and also desirable for gaining wisdom, she took some and ate it. She also gave some to her husband, who was with her, and he ate it. Then the eyes of both of them were opened, and they realized they were naked; so they sewed fig leaves together and made coverings for themselves.

*Damaged goods, defiled, devalued, broken, used, not good enough, overlooked, unworthy, forgotten, lost, invisible, unseen, stained, tainted, unimportant, rejected, ashamed, hidden, a zero, unloved; God doesn't love me. God is mad at me. Where are you, God? Why didn't you stop this from happening to me? Why didn't you protect me? You are the all-powerful, all-knowing God. Didn't you know this would happen?* I remember when I told and asked myself these things, over and over again. I grew up believing in and praying to God, yet the devil's whispers shouted, overpowering God's voice to me. I think back at being the tender age of only four years old. I remember that happy little girl playing with her dolls, playing at the park, Mommy and Daddy doing all the right things to protect me. We were always just happy with the simple things in life. Until all of that happiness and innocence had been snatched away from me. Let me take you back to a very long time ago…

It was a pleasant Friday morning. Daddy had taken that day off from work. Mom helped me get dressed. I wore a lovely red-and-white dress with frilly white ankle socks and black patent-leather Mary-Jane style shoes. That day was my first preschool play. We were so excited. Daddy wore a dress jacket, dress shirt, and nice slacks. You would think he was going to a big important event, like a wedding or something. But indeed, for Mom and Dad, this was an important event. My very first play, ever. I had memorized all of the words to "I'm a Little Teapot." How proud I was to know all of the words to that song. What a sense of accomplishment for me. Mom and Dad were sitting in the front row of the classroom. Mom's eyes watered with gleam and Daddy's smile went from ear to ear, his camera ready in his hand. My classmates and I wore little teapot costumes that we made out of big cardboard, and we painted pastel-colored little faces on them. The best part of preparing for the play was painting the teapot faces. After all, I loved painting and Mom said I was the artist in our family. After weeks of practice and preparation, the performance had been over just like that. Me and my group of preschool friends stood in front of a bunch of clapping, whistling, and proud parents. Camera flashes blinded us. It was such a good morning. Little did I know that it would be one of the last moments of pure joy before evil suddenly introduced itself to me. It was an evil that would take residence into my undefiled life.

"Natasha, you were really good, Honey. I'm so proud of you," Daddy said as he picked me up and hugged me tight.

I smiled shyly as I held onto him tightly, too.

"We have a little surprise for you," Mom said.

"What is it?"

"Take a guess," Daddy said.

"You got me a Snickers bar?"

"No," laughed Mom.

"We are going to take you to your favorite place to eat," Daddy said with a smile.

"Yay! Mama's Little Italy?" I yelped.

"Yes! And you can order whatever you want, Sweetheart."

I could taste those chocolate chip cannolis. It was like they had just told me I was going to Disney.

"Auntie Lucy and Uncle Joseph are also visiting later on."

"And my cousins, too?" I asked.

"Of course silly. Joe Jr. and Lisa are both coming."

This day had been close to perfect. And it hadn't been over just yet. I couldn't wait for my cousins to come visit. I'm an only child, so my cousins were the next best thing to having a brother and sister. My cousin Lisa was a year younger than me. We were very close, like sisters. My cousin Joe Jr. was sixteen, almost seventeen years old. Joe loved to prank people. He was what everyone called "the bad kid." I just thought that's how older boy cousins were supposed to be. He didn't faze me.

Early evening had then arrived. The sun's face was a deep mandarin-orange color with pink clouds hiding behind it. I watched it slowly settling down from my bedroom window. Then I heard the doorbell.

"Mommy, Mommy, I think they're here!"

Daddy opened the door, and Lisa bolted toward me and we wrapped our arms around each other.

"Let's go play tea time!" Lisa smiled.We didn't waste any time. We scurried away quickly into to my bedroom. I could smell the yummy food lingering in the halls. Mom prepared the breaded chicken cutlets and had just added the fresh mozzarella and homemade sauce on top. Chicken parmigiana was Dad's favorite.

I had a knack for being able to pay attention to my surroundings while busy doing something else. I could hear the laughter of my parents, auntie, and uncle from the kitchen. The evening was perfect. Then my bedroom door creaked as it slowly opened.

"Hey!" Joe shouted and then laughed obnoxiously. "What are you two brats doing?"

"We are having a tea party," I said."Yeah, we are having a tea party. Do you want some tea, Joe?" Lisa asked in her babyish voice.

"Tea? There is no tea in there. What kind of boring game is this?" Joe said.

Tears welled up in Lisa's eyes, and she suddenly ran out, crying. "Daddy, Joe is being mean again."

Joe just laughed, without a care in the world.

"Joe!" Uncle Joseph yelled. "What did you do now?"

"I didn't do anything. I'm just joking around with them."

I just dismissed the whole thing. I figured, even in my little four-year-old mind, that Lisa was only still a baby, and maybe she just needed to sleep. After all, she was only three years old. I consoled her and we continued to play. After some time later, Little Lisa fell asleep on my bed.

I started feeling a little sleepy myself, so I laid next to her and dozed off. It didn't seem that I had been asleep that long, when I felt something weird. *Was I dreaming?* But then the feeling became more profound. As my eyes lazily opened, I could see that Joe was sitting at the edge of my bed. His hand had a tight grip on my inner thigh. It kind of hurt.

"Argh!" I screamed.

"Shhhh! Be quiet," Joe whispered, placing his hand over my mouth.

"Nooo!"

Lisa woke up crying hysterically. My happy room, which had been filled with laughter earlier, suddenly became a room of fear.

The door swiftly opened.

"What's going on? What's wrong, Honey?" Mom asked worriedly.

"Ummm, I'm sorry. The girls were sleeping. I guess Natasha saw my shadow and got scared," Joe explained.

"Is that what happened, Baby? Are you, okay?" Mom asked again.

"Ah, yes, Mommy," I said, confused.

At this point, the only thing that made sense in my little mind was that I had a nightmare.

Auntie Lucy rushed in. "What did you do, Joe?"

"Why do you think I did anything, Mom? Nothing! I did nothing!" Joe argued.

Auntie Lucy quickly picked up Lisa and embraced her. "I think we better get going. It's getting late," she said.Little Lisa's head rested on my auntie's shoulder. Mom followed them out.

Joe followed behind my mom. He turned around and locked eyes with me as he smirked, and rested his forefinger on the top of his lips. "Shhhhhhh." Then he walked out.

Still confused about what just happened, I laid down on my bed wide awake. I tried to replay it in my mind. After much thinking, I reasoned with myself that I had dreamed the whole thing. After all, my cousin Joe had always been annoying, and maybe that's why I dreamed that he was trying to hurt me.

## CHAPTER TWO

# Let Me Introduce You to Fear

Proverbs 4:16–18

For they cannot rest until they do evil; they are robbed of sleep till they make someone stumble.

They eat the bread of wickedness and drink the wine of violence. The path of the righteous is like the morning sun, shining ever brighter till the full light of day.

The dreary clouds danced in the sky; behind them hid the hazy sun. The windows perspired with condensation. It had been a few days since we'd seen my auntie and uncle. It was unusual, especially for Auntie Lucy, because she'd always stop by to visit Mom. They only lived about five minutes away and both had a close-sister bond. Mom and Auntie Lucy are Irish twins, only eleven months apart. Some people believed they were really identical twins because they looked so much alike. Both of them have light-brown, curly hair with natural highlight streaks, hazel eyes, and light-brown skin complexion. They were a mix between my grandpa and Nana. Nana was a beautiful African-American woman with bright green eyes and Grandpa, a handsome Puerto Rican man with coffee-brown eyes. Quite often, when I walk with Dad anywhere, they'd ask him who I belonged to. Daddy would laugh each time. I'm guessing because Dad is Irish with blue eyes. I am a mini version of Mom, though, and I felt lucky to have Nana's green eyes, too. Daddy always said I would never have a boyfriend. Otherwise, they'd have to go through him. Ha! He had always been so protective of me.

Later that Wednesday afternoon, there was a loud knock on the door. Mom quickly walked toward the door, hoping it was Auntie Lucy.

Mom looked surprised. "Hey! Joe. How's it going, Sweetheart? Where are your mom and Lisa?"

"She took Lisa for a follow up to the pediatrician. She had some sort of rash on one side of her face," Joe replied. "And Dad is still at work."

"Oh no, what sort of rash?"

"Mom seems to think it's some kind of allergic reaction. She sent me over here and asked if I can wait here until she's done and that she'll be right over after the appointment."

"Of course you can. No wonder I haven't seen her. I'm cooking my famous garlic mashed potatoes, corn on the cob, collard greens, and Uncle Phillip is grilling some steaks. I've been calling your mom the last couple of days, and no answer."

"Something was wrong with our phone. But it's fixed now," Joe explained."Hey, since you're here, is it okay if you stay here for a few minutes with Natasha?"

"Sure, Auntie," Joe quickly replied.

"I'm going to run out and buy a couple more steaks since I know you guys are staying over for dinner tonight. I'll be right back."

"No problem, Auntie Lorraine."

I just continued painting. Mom bought me a few canvases and a cool new palette of paint. Since I had just started painting the magical garden, while overhearing Mom and Joe's conversation, I decided that I would add a little girl in the garden that represented Little Lisa. I wanted to paint something that would cheer her up. I got lost in the painting. I envisioned Little Lisa running across the beautiful forest-green lawn toward the colorful, magical garden. The garden had the most exotic flowers in it. Flowers that I don't think even existed in real life. There were neon-pink peonies that were treelike in size and iridescent white orchids with swirls of bright purple streaks. The orchids looked like jumbo umbrellas.

In the garden, there were also oversized fruit. Beautiful fruit! Giant cherry-red apples and tall cucumbers surrounded by sunshine-yellow tulips. It was a garden wonderland. My imagination continued to run wild. I wanted to live in this wondrous, bright, and fruitful garden. Abruptly, a monstrous thick, black cloud slowly began hovering over the garden with the little girl in it. Joe walked up right beside me and pushed me slightly.

"What are you painting there, you Little Runt?"

"I am painting a magical garden," I replied. "And I'm going to paint Lisa in it and give it to her when I finish."

"That painting is kinda boring...gardens are boring. Why don't you draw something more interesting, like something creepy or scary?" Joe said as he smirked.

"Scary? I don't like scary things."

He picked me up from the stool. I became a little startled since he'd never done that before.

"What are you doing?" I asked. "I'm still painting."

"Well, I figured you'd be more comfortable if you sat on my lap while you paint. Besides, I'd like to look at it from your point of view," Joe said.

Although still confused, in my little mind at the time, I just went along with it. I didn't want him to get more annoying than he already was.

He abruptly sat me on his lap. I immediately felt uncomfortable and realized I wouldn't really be able to paint this way.

"Joe, I want to sit by myself."

"Aww, come on. It's okay. Just try…I won't bother you," Joe said, giving me a devilish smile.There I sat on his lap, thinking and wondering when Daddy would be done. I could hear the lawn mower still going, so loud, in the backyard. As I started to continue painting, Joe kept moving, fidgeting around and wouldn't stop. I didn't understand what he was trying to do. His arms were folded across the top of my lap. I couldn't move.

"Joe!" I yelled. "It's bothering me."

But Joe kept silent. The more I talked, the tighter his arms pressed against my lap. My heart pounded in my little chest. My breaths became harder as if I couldn't breathe. I yelled out again. But still, not a word out of him. His arms were hurting me. The front doorknob started turning and I heard a clicking noise. Quickly, Joe jumped off the stool, pushing me off at the same time. I fell sideways onto the floor and began crying. My hip hurt so badly from the slight fall.

"What in the world happened?" Mom yelled as she placed the grocery bag on the counter. She had returned from the store.

But I couldn't stop crying.

"Uhh…" Joe looked scared.

"What happened?" Mom shouted again.

"I…I just picked her up to move her," Joe explained. "It was an accident."

"So you dropped her!? Why did you try moving her in the first place? Joe! I leave you here for a few minutes and this is what happens!? Just please go over there." Mom fumed. She picked me up.

"Baby, are you okay? Mommy is here."

Her hug felt so safe. The energy in my body felt drained. It was a feeling I had never experienced before. It was pure fear. I didn't quite understand why I felt so afraid. It didn't make sense. And why was Joe acting so weird with me? Why did he remain silent while pressing onto me so tightly? I thought maybe he didn't like me and tried to scare me.

"What happened baby?"

"Joe… Joe…" I muttered nervously.

"Joe what, Honey?" Mom stared him down.

"Joe scared me."

"How did I scare you? She's lying!" Joe screamed.

"Hey, hey," Mom interrupted.

Then Daddy walked in. "Hey, what's going on in here?"

I ran into Daddy's arms with my head in his chest.

"Joe picked her up and somehow dropped her!" Mom said.

"You what?" Dad said with angry eyes toward Joe.

"It was an accident! I swear! I'm sorry. I told Natasha that her painting was boring and that maybe she could paint something scary. I was only kidding."

"Well, I'm going to have a talk with your mom when she gets here. You need to apologize to Natasha," Mom, said upset.

"I'm sorry, Natasha," mumbled Joe.

I just nodded. Looking back, I realize now I could not express myself to my parents. I didn't quite understand what had happened. All I know is that it didn't feel good to me. For the first time, I had seen Joe through a completely different lens. He had always been the annoying big cousin, but this time, I'd seen him as somewhat of a threat. Maybe something was wrong with me. Maybe in my four-year-old little mind, I had perceived something that wasn't real. Maybe what I sensed was just a figment of my imagination. All I know is that fear had introduced itself to me for the first time that day.

## CHAPTER THREE

# THE MONSTER IN THE GARDEN

MATTHEW 6:13

And lead us not into temptation, but deliver us from the evil one.

Finally, the sky opened up as the clouds eventually disappeared. The rest of that evening turned out fine. Although, whenever no one was looking, Joe gave me haughty eyes. It looked like he was upset and I didn't understand why. The next few weeks after that were a blur. Mom's new schedule as sergeant at the precinct had been crazy. And Dad's hours at the hospital were all over the place. But we were looking forward to the upcoming camping trip. It was tradition for both of our families to go camping every year, around the middle of May. We had also become friendly with other families who'd stay at the same camp grounds. Mom never liked the whole camping outside in the tents thing, so we'd rent these really cool log cabins that had bathrooms and a kitchen. Little Lisa and I would take turns having sleepovers in each of our family's cabins.

The weekend before the camping trip, Dad had set up the lemonade stand in his old neighborhood in the Bronx, like he did last year. It had been such a success that Dad decided we'd do it every year as a tradition. Mom made two big pitchers of regular lemonade and two big pitchers of pink lemonade. My lemonade stand sign was really pretty and creative. Mom designed the lettering on the words and I painted pink and bright-yellow lemon trees all over the poster sign. We were charging twenty-five cents for a small and fifty cents for a large. Dad had always worked the lemonade stand with me.

I could see from down the street two young girls approaching. They were about seventeen or eighteen years old. Something about them didn't look right. They looked a bit disheveled, dressed provocatively, and wore slightly smeared makeup. It almost looked like they had been clubbing and broke night or something. I felt sorry for them. As they approached, I could see one girl whispering to the other.

"Lemonade, come get your lemonade," I said loud and proud.

"Hey, do you give out free cups of the lemonade? You know, like for a free sample?" one of the girls asked.

"Not really," Dad quickly responded.

"You can buy a small one. It's only twenty-five cents," I said to her.

"Ah. Nah. It's okay. We don't have any money on us."

I looked up at Dad and I motioned with my finger for him to bend down toward me. I whispered in his ear, "Daddy, I want to give them both a cup of lemonade for free. Can I? Pretty please?"

Dad just smiled at me and nodded.

"Which one do you want? You can have the bigger cup for free."

"Really?"

"Yes," I said with a big smile. My heart felt happy.

"You are a special little girl. God bless you."

The other girl took a sip. "Oooh, so good."

She kind of reminded me of Mom's side of the family. She was really pretty, with black, curly hair and beautiful caramel skin. But behind her lovely smile appeared a deep sadness in her eyes.

"Hey! Hey! I've been looking for the two of you!" It was a burly man, who was wearing dark shades. He shouted at them as he drove up in his black Chevy suburban truck.

The girls looked nervous and hopped right in the car. The car then peeled off. The man scared me.

"Daddy, who was that?"

"I don't know, Sweetheart. But I didn't get a good feeling about him. And the poor girls look like they have been stained."

I didn't know it at that time, but the two girls were prostitutes and the man had been their pimp. I also had no idea what Dad meant when he said that the two girls were stained. I thought he meant their clothing was dirty, or stained like with paint. Often the way my hands would stain after doing one of my paintings.

The week had gone by so quickly. I thought, *Thank God!* Camping time had arrived. I couldn't wait. Our camping trips were always so much fun. We arrived on a Friday night and didn't do much other than unpack, ate, and showered. Everyone had been pretty tired, so bedtime was early. Lucky for me, Little Lisa slept over in our cabin that night. The next morning was Saturday, May 18, 1974. What a beautiful morning it had been. I could smell the pancakes that Mom had on the skillet. The bacon smelled yummy, too. I could hear them sizzling in the pan. My stomach began growling, crying out for breakfast. Before we headed to the kitchen, I opened the window curtain and watched the yellow-orange sky become brighter. The sounds of the baby birds were so beautiful. It was going to be a great weekend.

After a full day of swimming, barbecuing, eating, laughing, and playing, dinnertime had soon arrived. The families always put together a buffet-style setting with a variety of dishes cooked by each family. Dad and Uncle Joseph started a fire so all of us could make s'mores. I ate so much that night, I felt like my belly was going to pop. It was my turn that Saturday night to sleep over with Little Lisa in her cabin.

Our parents were still outside by the campfire. Little Lisa and I were in our pajamas, playing with our dolls. Their cabin had been a lot bigger than the one we were in. So we were in heaven. There were so many rooms. At least that's how we perceived it. There was a big back room on the second level. In the room were two twin-size beds. It was a beautiful, rustic room with boxed wooden ceilings. It had been a very active, busy day. Little Lisa fell asleep. I could still hear Mom and Dad outside with the other adults. There were quite a few teens, too. My eyes grew heavy with sleep. I prayed the Lord's Prayer in my mind like I did every night with Mom and Dad. After a while, I heard Auntie Lucy and Mom walk in to check on us and kiss us. Although my eyes were closed, I could tell that the room turned pitch black after the sound of the light switch clicked. The door then closed. I had been in the most peaceful and deepest slumber ever, until it was interrupted. The floor creaked. I opened my eyes slightly and saw a shadowy dark figure. I gasped. Quickly the dark figure ran up to me, but before I could scream his hand covered my mouth. My little heart pounded hard in my chest. There was a full moon out that night, so I could see the bright light shining through the slightly opened curtain. It was then that I recognized his eyes.

"Shhhhhhh!" Joe whispered. "It's me, Joe. Don't be scared."

But I was scared.

Joe softly ran his fingers through my hair from the top of my head. I felt so tired. I just let him do it. But then, his hand touched my shoulder and slowly rubbed his hand down my arm.

"What are you doing?" I whispered.

"Shhhhhh," he said again. "No talking. If you talk, you're going to wake Lisa up and then you'll get in a lot of trouble. So no talking. Okay?"

"Okay," I said, confused and half asleep. I started to feel a little nauseous and my heart wouldn't stop beating so fast. I didn't feel so good.

Joe's hand now landed on my belly, moving farther down.

All I could say was, "No." I kept whispering, "No..."

Whenever I painted, I would imagine being and getting lost in the painting. In my little mind, I thought if I just closed my eyes it would all go away, that he would go away. Maybe I was in a bad dream. I thought that with my eyes closed, I could run away into another time or dimension, just as I had done with each of my paintings. The uncomfortable touch wasn't going away, either. With my eyes closed, I envisioned myself again in the colorful, magical garden. The thick, black cloud that hovered over the garden suddenly turned into the shape of a big monster. The monster began chasing me in the garden. The beautiful, tall neon-pink peonies were wilted, frail, and shriveled. Everything that the gardener had planted in my garden suddenly died. The soil was hard and cracked. The monster roared. I ran and ran, panting and soon running out of breath. I tripped and fell from the deep, open cracks in the soil. Before I could get up, the big monster grabbed me. I couldn't breathe. I cried hard silently. I screamed out, but without sound. Almost as if someone had pressed the mute button on. The tears flowed down my face. The monster had constricted my breathing. I felt as if my heart caved into my chest. I heard the monster speak. His calm voice did not match his hideous face.

"Natasha, you are like a pretty flower," he said in his deep, ugly voice.

At that very moment I, too, began to wither and shrivel. The peony and I were just alike. We were both once colorful and vibrant, now without color or life. The monster placed his hand over my mouth firmly as I fell into unconsciousness. I could see myself falling, spiraling down through a big hole in the ground.

"Natasha… Natasha, Sweetheart?"

I opened my eyes. It was Auntie Lucy.

"Sweetheart, are you okay?" she asked.

I covered my eyes with one arm. The room had been so bright. The sun shone in. Confusion set in. I realized it had already been morning time. My head pounded and my body felt sore.

"You looked like you've been crying, Sweetheart? Are you okay?" Auntie Lucy asked.

But I just cried and cried. "I want to go with Mommy and Daddy," I sobbed.

"Aww, Love, did you have a nightmare? I made you girls your favorite, pancakes," she replied.

"I want to go with Mommy and Daddy." Inconsolably, I continued to sob.

"Okay, okay. Come on, let's go." She picked me up and carried me in her arms.

The weeks that followed were long and drawn out for me. I didn't want to go to school anymore. Fear weighed heavily on me. I didn't want Mom to leave my side. Each time she and Dad had to get ready for work, I would lose it. They didn't understand what was happening to me. I continued to have nightmares about that last night at the camping trip. I told Mom about the monster in the garden that hurt me. But she continued to assure me that it was only a nightmare. She also knew how much I loved to paint and wondered why I hadn't picked up a paintbrush since the camping trip. I feared I would slip into the garden with the monster in it. I didn't want him to hurt me again. I didn't want to feel that uncomfortable, painful touch again.

## CHAPTER FOUR

# CURSED SUMMER

PROVERBS 6:12–19

A troublemaker and a villain, who goes about with a corrupt mouth, who winks maliciously with his eye, signals with his feet and motions with his fingers, who plots evil with deceit in his heart—he always stirs up conflict. Therefore disaster will overtake him in an instant; he will suddenly be destroyed—without remedy. There are six things the Lord hates, seven that are detestable to him: haughty eyes, a lying tongue, hands that shed innocent blood, a heart that devises wicked schemes, feet that are quick to rush into evil, a false witness who pours out lies and a person who stirs up conflict in the community.

Summer of 1974:

The blazing-hot sun pierced through the cloudless, ocean-blue sky. Buzzing bees and radiant butterflies swirled through the air. The days of the sun kissing our faces, fresh lemon iced tea and beach time had arrived. Kids rode their bikes, while others played basketball. Mom had taken a few weeks off from work to stay home with me. She thought maybe I had been acting out because of lack of quality time with her. She acknowledged that as an only child, it can be lonely for me at times. And after all, Mom being a wife, mother, and cop, could also prove a challenging schedule. She had no clue that it had nothing to do with any of that. It came time for her to go back to work soon. I was mortified. Even though my babysitter was a wonderful older woman, Beth, who was like a grandmother to me, it still wasn't the same. I just didn't want Mom to leave me. "Mommy, I wish you could stay home with me forever."

"I know, Honey. I'm so sorry. If I don't go to work, then we can't live in our nice house. Daddy and I work hard for us to live happy and comfortable. But I promise on our days off, we will do fun stuff together like we always do. Okay?" Mom smiled.

"Okay," I agreed reluctantly, my head down.

"Tasha, why don't you paint something for me? Why don't you finish painting your garden?"

*"Tasha"* had been Mom's nickname for me.

I thought maybe I should start painting again. Maybe Mom was right. So I started painting my garden. I picked up where I left off. The last time, I had added my cousin Lisa in it. My paintbrush hit the canvas again. As I painted and looked at it, suddenly a force pulled me into my imagination again. Instead of seeing the bright, beautiful flowers and the magical giant fruit, all I could see was the big, black cloud. The hideous monster appeared again and brought me back to that room in the log cabin. The monster began chasing me once more. Only this time, his rage caused him to develop three heads. And instead of two arms and hands, he then had six arms and hands. I started screaming.

"Tasha!" Mom grabbed me.

There I sat in the living room with the paintbrush in my hand. Mom gasped and I didn't know why.

"Oh, my goodness, Tasha. What is this?" She pointed at my painting.

To my horror, the garden that was once so colorful and bright became so dark and messy. In the middle of all the vibrant colors was a blob of black and a repulsive face in the middle of it. I couldn't believe what my hand had just painted.

"What's wrong, Honey?" Mom worriedly asked. "I've never seen you paint anything like this before."

But I didn't answer. I couldn't answer. I had been too afraid. I thought that if I told her about the monster again from that night in the log cabin, he would soon follow me from my paintings and into my dreams.

Mom hugged me tight. "Mommy is here and will always be here with you. If something is bothering you, you can tell me, Sweetheart."

But I didn't tell her. In fact, I never spoke about the monster to her or to anyone, ever again. The secret had been between me and the monster forever. He told me if I ever told Mom or anyone else about him, that he would kill me.

Mom was able to extend her stay at home another week. But that week just flew by. Dad's shifts at the hospital were so long. It was a very hot day in the end of July. Beth had made yummy homemade lemonade. She knew that was one of my favorite drinks. It had been weeks since I'd seen my cousin Joe. But this day, he'd gotten off from his summer job at the camp early. He decided to stop by. The doorbell rang. My babysitter Beth answered the door.

"Hey, Joe. How's it going, Buddy?"

"I'm great, Beth."

"What brings you here today? Your aunt and uncle aren't here."

"I just stopped by to see Natasha. I've been so busy with work and just miss my little cousin," Joe explained while looking at me.

My heart felt like it was trying to pierce through my chest. My legs were wobbly and my hands couldn't stop shaking.

"What's the matter, Sweetheart?" Beth asked me.

But I just froze. I didn't know what to say to her.

She instantly hugged me. "Oh, my goodness. You're shaking."

I held her tight, hoping that she'd take that as a sign not to leave me alone with Joe.

Joe quickly interrupted.

"Aww, come here, Natasha."

But I wouldn't let go of Beth.

Beth asked if I was feeling sick. I shrugged my shoulders as to suggest, "I don't know."

Joe gave me a hard look as he smiled at the same time, then he said, "Ah, she's okay, Beth. I think she's just being shy. It's been a few weeks since I'd seen my little cousin. You go on ahead and finish whatever you were doing. I'll cheer her up."

"Natasha, I'm just going to finish up a few things here in the kitchen. I'll fix you up a peanut butter and jelly sandwich after I'm done. Just the way you like it. Okay?"

Discouraged, I just nodded and softly said, "Okay."

When Beth returned to the kitchen, Joe grabbed my hand and motioned me to walk with him. "Come on, show me the paintings in your room."

"No. I don't want to."

But he didn't take no for an answer. I started crying inside. I could feel my tears welling up in my eyes. I heard in my head, *Natasha, you are such a pretty flower.* It was the monster's voice talking to me.

My mind was fuzzy.

The next thing I knew we were in my bedroom upstairs. It had been bright and sunny outside, yet all I could see was gloom and pitch darkness. Heaviness came over me. Joe gently laid me down on my bed. Then there he appeared again. It was the monster. My bed wasn't a bed and I wasn't in my room anymore. It was a dark ditch inside the garden. The tall trees hovered over me like big creatures covering me with their long, curly, creepy arms that were their branches.

The monster said, "Shhh, it's okay. Do not be afraid. Do not talk or scream. It'll be over before you know it. If you talk, you'll get in big trouble."

My eyes shut tight. I couldn't see and was terrified. Whimpering, I told the monster to stop. But he just couldn't help himself. My entire being, existence, and all consciousness went hazy as I laid in the dark ditch inside the garden. A garden that had once been my sanctuary had now become my living hell.

## CHAPTER FIVE

# THE NIGHT MY SOUL DIED

JOHN 3:20

Everyone who does evil hates the light, and will not come into the light for fear that their deeds will be exposed.

The next five years dragged on and my nine-year-old self continued to dwell in that dark, transcendent garden. The colorful, beaming garden full of life that my paintbrush had once reflected back when I was a little girl had been dried up, not watered, or nurtured at all. It transformed itself into pure torment. I learned over time to hide my pain. I learned to live with this secret that had been eating me alive. I had developed the art of escape through my paintings, in order to remove myself from the painful reality. As long as Mom and Dad remained jubilant, and we were that happy family everyone thought we were, I needed to continue going on with the facade. Mom and Dad were my peace, my sanctuary, but even then I knew they couldn't save me. I prayed every night and asked God to take the monster away. I prayed for him to disappear. And as I endured the habitual abuse, I even prayed for the monster to die. But he just wouldn't go away.

*God, are you there? Can you hear my prayers? Why won't you take this monster away from me?* I thought and asked these questions over and over again.

Somehow, even throughout all of the insanity, I still believed God had been with me the whole time. I would get upset at myself sometimes for not blaming God. One thing I knew for sure is that I couldn't stop praying or believing. It's the only thing I had left. With each year that passed, I believed it would be the year that God would remove the monster. But the monster still remained.

The evening had been like something out of a winter wonderland. The deep, dark-green pine trees were perfectly capped with bright white snow. The big, beautiful snowflakes slowly dropped from the sky like fluffy feathers. It was Mom's annual Christmas party at work. Dad always went with her every year. Mom always looked so beautiful. That night, she wore a long, red halter-style gown. She looked a lot like Nana; her beauty was natural. I do remember the red lipstick and her long, lush lashes that night. Mom was so excited, but little did she know that my demise awaited me. Auntie Lucy and Uncle Joseph always babysat me. Joe had just turned twenty-one and still lived with them. I prayed he'd be out with his friends that night. Dad had driven me to Auntie's house to drop me off. When we arrived, my worst fear became true. Joe had been right there, almost as if he'd been waiting for me. Little Lisa wasn't so little anymore. She was so happy I was there with her. Lisa was like my little sister, so I had been very protective of her. I always wondered if Joe had been bad to her, too. I couldn't even imagine it because Lisa always seemed so happy. But then again, so did I. I had learned over the years to hide it well. I learned how to play pretend really well. It pained me to imagine that Lisa had been living in that dark garden just like me. I didn't want to think about it anymore. I couldn't ask her if he was, because if he weren't hurting her, then she'd wonder why I asked such an outrageous question.

Here I went again. I waved good-bye to Dad as if it were going to be the last time I saw him. I ran up to him and latched my arms around him really tightly.

"Tasha, Honey…" he chuckled. "I'll be back to pick you up in the morning. I'm not leaving you forever you know."

"Okay, Daddy. I love you and Mom."

"I know, Sweetheart. So do we." He looked at me with endearment.

Auntie Lucy had cooked one of my favorite foods, fried chicken, homemade garlic mashed potatoes, and corn on the cob.

"Come on, guys. Just served dinner," Auntie said.

"Umm, I'm not really hungry," I replied."What? Natasha! What's the matter? You must not be feeling well. This is your favorite."

But she had no idea that I felt sick to my stomach. I felt uneasy not knowing if Joe had his plot against me in order. I had no desire to eat. So I went along with what Auntie said.

"Yes, Auntie Lucy. My stomach feels a little weird. Maybe I'll eat later."

"Not sure how much later, Sweetheart. It's already six thirty," Auntie said with concern.

"It's okay, Auntie. I'll sit with you all at the table."

I kept looking around for Joe. He'd slipped away. I prayed in my mind, hoping that he had planned on staying out all night. After dinner, Lisa and I played together. We painted and did arts and crafts, too. It appeared I would be in the clear. Joe had indeed stepped out. It turned out to be a peaceful night with my cousin. I slept in Lisa's room. They always kept an extra little bed in there for me. After all, it was practically my second home. Lisa had always been a heavy sleeper. I envied the fact that she had the natural ability to fall asleep so quickly. I couldn't do that. My mind had been a residence for ideas and thoughts of worry and fear. After praying, I looked out the window and just watched the majestic snowfall. The wintery December night appeared perfect. My heart jumped when I heard the door opening.

*Oh no*! I thought. Inside my mind, I screamed, *God, no! Please no! I can't take this anymore!* My mind ran into escape mode as I saw the monster enter the room. He slowly walked toward me. Only this time, he grabbed my hand tightly, forcing me to walk out of the room with him. Everyone had been asleep in the house. Joe's room was downstairs.

My head continued to swing no. But no was not an answer the monster would ever accept. His long, creepy finger placed over his mouth to suggest for me to be quiet. I cried silently as the tears poured out of my eyes and flooded down my face. We soon entered his room. The monster's face was grotesque. Slimy, thick saliva was dripping off his fangs. In the murky garden, it also snowed, only the snow was pitch black.

In his chilling voice he said, "Natasha, you are a beautiful flower," as he'd always say to me. I started running through the dead flowers that were as tall as cornstalks. I tried getting lost in it like a maze. The rotten giant fruit had a horrible stench. My breath was short and my energy was on low battery. It was inevitable. The monster was bigger, faster, and stronger. He then caught up to me, grabbed me, picked me up, and tossed my tiny body onto the muddy, soiled ground. His sharp claws shredded through my pajamas. It was frigid and I couldn't stop trembling.

"Please don't hurt me anymore," I pleaded with the monster.But he looked at me like a lion ready to devour his prey. He had been too hungry and needed to satisfy his appetite. As I lie on the ground crying, the monster began to mar me. The pain had been agonizing and pierced right to my soul. I envisioned my spirit lift up from my flesh and hovered over me. It was the happy me; there was light surrounding my spirit. I looked so refreshed, clean, and full of joy. My undefiled spirit had been staring down at a girl who was officially mangled, defaced, and physically vandalized. My flesh was alive, my heart was still beating strong, but my emotional soul had died. For the first time in my young life, I didn't feel the presence of God. After his belly was full, I crouched into fetal position in that dead and dark garden. I'd given up. I prayed aloud, "God, please take me. I don't want to live anymore." I looked at the monster and said to him, "Just kill me."

But he didn't kill me physically. His carnal, evil appetite had stolen, killed, and destroyed my innocence forever.

## CHAPTER SIX

# BAD HABITS

1 CORINTHIANS 15:33

Do not be misled: "Bad company corrupts good character."

In the year of 1986, autumn had brought forth cool breezes and warm, earthy foliage. It was the season of pumpkins, tasty apple cider, and hot apple pie. The leaves were an artful array of brimstone reds, yellows, and golds, the color of beeswax, and bright amber hues. Children were starting their new routines as school had been back in session. I was sixteen and beginning eleventh grade. This would have been a year when many girls my age would have been excited about—sweet sixteens, junior proms, and college hunting. But none of those things mattered to me. I didn't have a sweet sixteen because I didn't want one. In fact, I didn't even want to go to school anymore. My poor parents had worked so hard to raise me right, to instill God and faith in my foundation, yet there I was, a very damaged girl. And despite their efforts, they couldn't figure out why. Mom and Dad had taken me to see child psychologists in the last few years. But the doctors couldn't break me. They couldn't get any truth out of me. By that time, I had been filled with too much shame and fear. I thought it had been too late for me. No one could fix me. The monster and I had a repulsive secret that needed to be taken to my grave. The night my soul died at the age of nine took a turn for the worse. It had showed up in my lack of enthusiasm for life, school, friends, art, or play. The year that the monster stripped my soul away from me, my cousin Joe had finally gone away. He joined the army soon after. I had prayed over the years relentlessly for the monster to disappear, but by the time that prayer was finally answered, the damage that had been done to me, was too great for me to handle. I beat myself up for not abandoning God and my belief in Him even though, deep down inside, I almost believed the lie that I had been abandoned by Him. I knew in my spirit that it couldn't be true. I believed that God had been with me, but still couldn't understand what took Him so long to remove the monster out of my life. Even though God removed the monster out of my presence physically, the monster continued to haunt me in my daily thoughts, in my dreams at night and in my spirit. I had also developed the curse of insomnia. I refused to close my eyes because the monster's torment had become more constant and relentless. In the past, I feared this would happen to me, and now my fear came true. Faith no longer resided in my heart. Faith had been evicted out of me by sheer terror.

It had been a few weeks before my junior prom. Mom kept insisting that I go and even went as far as buying me a really pretty dress. But I dreaded being around people. A senior told me about a kid in our school who sold pills. He sold mostly Valium and Xanax. She'd told me he was stealing them from home and selling them. Supposedly, his dad was a pharmacist. Reluctantly, that summer before school started, I took on a part-time job at our local deli. So I could afford to start this new secret habit. A habit that I thought could possibly help me escape my pain. My paintings were no longer an escape into a blissful abyss, but rather a never-ending affliction. The first time I took one of those pills, I couldn't believe how this tiny, little thing had so much influence over me. I imag ined myself on a beautiful white cloud in the bluest sky ever. I could see down below me the tiny images of the world. But to my amazement, there it was...the beautiful, bright, colorful garden that I once imagined I lived in so long ago as a little child. Oh, how wonderful! There was no monster present, there was no darkness...I found it! I found the answer to finding my peace. Oh, this wonderful pill! It became the answer to all of my problems. It was the beginning of allowing the devil's lies into my spirit, little by little. It was the lie that anything else except Jesus could be the answer to all my problems.

I grew an addiction to pain pills too.

"Tasha! Tasha!" Mom kept calling out for me.

Even though I could hear her, she had no clue that I was completely out of it upstairs.

I just could not get up.

My door quickly opened.

"Tasha! What are you doing still sleeping?" Mom said while opening up my blinds.

"Mom, please... I told you that I don't feel good."

"Oh, no, you don't. You can't keep doing this, Sweetheart. C'mon. Get up, wash up, and you'll feel better after you eat," Mom said desperately.

"I can't eat, Mom."

"I don't like the way you look. I think I'm taking you to the doctor," she said.

"No, please. It's just that time of the month for me, Mom. My cramps are bad," I lied. I couldn't take the chance that I'd get a blood test and have my family find out I've been taking all kinds of pills. I couldn't control the new monster that had entered my life.

"All right, Love. I'll make you some tea and I'll bring you some Advil."

The phone rang. Mom came back into my bedroom. "Tasha, you have a phone call."

"Who is it, Mom?"

"She says her name is Cathy."

"Cathy?" I couldn't believe she actually called me. Cathy was considered one of the most popular girls in school. She was a senior at my high school, and a cheerleader. *Why is she calling me?* I thought. I got up and answered the phone. "Hello."

"Hi, Natasha. It's me…Cathy."

"Oh hey, Cathy."

"Listen, my parents are going away and I'm having a big party at my house next Saturday. You're invited."

"Party? Next weekend? Umm, I'm not sure. I'd love to go, but I have to ask my parents if it's okay." I was surprised.

"Aww, c'mon, it'll be a lot of seniors and the boys from the football team, too. It'll be fun. Why don't you ask them if you can sleepover? They don't need to know it's a party. Just in case they're strict or something."

"Wow. Okay. I'll let you know. Thanks for inviting me."

"Sure. Let me know soon, though, 'cause I need a head count."

"Okay."

"See ya," Cathy said.

As I put the phone down, I kept wondering, *Why me?* She wasn't really my friend. Although the senior who told me about the kid selling pills in school was actually Cathy's best friend. I thought maybe somehow I was "in" or maybe considered cool because I had become almost like one of them. Deep down inside, I didn't really want to go. Everyone thought I was pretty, but I didn't feel good about myself. Maybe if I went, I could start building up my confidence. After much thinking and contemplating, I thought, *Yes, I'll just go to the party. Now I just have to convince Mom and Dad that it is just a sleepover.*

## CHAPTER SEVEN

# New Monsters

Psalm 22:1

"My God, my God, why have you forsaken me? Why are you so far from my cries of anguish?"

The week before the party flew by. Saturday afternoon had soon arrived. I'd been able to convince Mom and Dad that it was only a sleepover. Cathy arranged a phone call earlier that week, from her parents to mine. They assured them it would be fine for me to stay over. What I didn't realize at the time was that Cathy's parents had no idea that she planned a party while they were away. I guess her parents really trusted her. After all, not only had she been popular in school, but she was also one of the smartest girls in school, too. Dad drove me to her house. When we pulled up to the address, we were stunned. Cathy practically lived in a mansion. The home looked like something out of a magazine. Did we have the right address? I thought. I still remember Dad's expression on his face.

"Sweetheart, are you sure we are at the right place?" he asked.

"I'm pretty sure, Dad. Her parents must be rich or something."

The landscaping in the front of the house had been something I'd always imagine in one of my paintings. There were beautiful flowers everywhere. It looked like a bright, floral wonderland. There were pillars at the end of the driveway with a tall, black gate. There was an intercom with what looked like a surveillance camera above it. Dad pressed the button.

A voice called out through the intercom, "Hi, Natasha." A buzzing noise sounded at the same time.

The black gate began opening.

"Wow," I said. "I wonder what her mom and dad do for a living."

"Tasha, remember what Mom and I told you. No going out without our permission. We agreed to the sleepover because we think it's good that you are going to have some fun time with a friend. Mom and I have been worried about you."

"I know, Dad. I will," I said with some guilt.

I really wanted to tell him about the party, but I didn't want Cathy getting in trouble. I'd also not be allowed to come to a party that wasn't supervised by parents. I knew I had to keep my mouth shut. If only I had known that it would be one of the biggest mistakes of my life.

Cathy had been waiting at the door to greet us. "Hello, Mr. McCarthy. Nice to meet you," she said to my dad.

"Hi, Cathy. It's nice to meet you, too." Dad shook her hand.

She smiled at us. "Come on in."

As we entered her home, we saw that the view inside was majestic. I'd never seen such high ceilings before. Hanging in the center of the ceiling was a gorgeous, gigantic chandelier. The floors were made of marble. It was absolutely breathtaking.

Dad looked around. "Are your parents here?"

"Umm, no. They stepped out. But I can have my mom or dad give you a call," Cathy said nervously.

"Yes, please. You girls aren't going anywhere, right? And, Tasha, you need to call me if you decide to go anywhere. We agreed to only a sleepover." Dad gave me a stern look.

"Dad!" I said. He was embarrassing me. "I know. Don't worry, Daddy."

"I'll be here at ten o'clock tomorrow morning to pick you up. We have church at eleven."

"Got it, Daddy." I kissed him on his cheek.

"Cathy, it was nice to meet you. Please ask your mom or dad to call me."

Cathy smiled. "Sure, Mr. McCarthy, I will. Thanks for letting Natasha sleep over."

Dad turned to me and said, "I'll speak to you later, Sweetheart."

"Okay, Dad."

He had a hard time leaving me.

Finally, Dad left. I looked out of the window and watched his silver BMW slowly drive off the property.

"Yay! You're free!" Cathy jumped up and down. "Aren't you excited?"

"Ah, yeah. I guess."

"Natasha, you have no clue how much fun we're going to have tonight."

"What about your parents? What if they call while the party is going on?" I asked worriedly.

Cathy laughed. "Natasha, Natasha…do you know how many times I've gotten away with this? Don't worry. My parents will never find out. I'm a good girl, so they think." She laughed and winked at me.

"What about my parents?" I asked.

"What about your parents?" she said sarcastically.

"Well, I know my dad. He won't rest unless your parents speak with him. He thought at least one of them would be home. I just don't want him coming back here and find us partying."

"Don't worry. I got you covered. Are you always like this?" Cathy chuckled, without a worry in the world.

"Actually, other than sleeping over my family's home, I've never had a sleepover with friends before."

"What!? Are you serious?" She looked shocked. "You poor thing," she added then laughed. "You've been seriously sheltered."

A couple of hours had passed. Cathy managed to have her mom call Dad. She explained to her mom we were just going to watch movies and do girl stuff. Now that that's out of the way, other kids already started to arrive at Cathy's house. She had me help her set up a bar table with all kinds of liquor. She also had a knack for preparing appetizers like mini sandwiches and some frozen finger foods I helped her bake earlier.

Before I knew it, the house was filled with teens everywhere. I'd gone upstairs to Cathy's bedroom to get the Valium out of my bag. I had it hidden in one of the pockets inside my jeans. A few hours into the party, Cathy and a bunch of her friends insisted I join in on the drinking game. I hadn't really drunk at all. They had no clue that I had taken my daily fix of pills. But afraid I wouldn't seem cool, I joined in on the drinking game. The whole football team was there. One of the football players kept giving me flirty eyes. He was tall with dark hair and brown eyes, and so handsome. I just pretended not to notice. Cathy tried playing Cupid.

"Natashaaaaa, guess what?" Cathy asked with a wide smile.

"What?"

"I think Jeremy likes you. Do you see the way he's been looking at you?"

"Umm, not really."

"Don't be shy. Go over there and talk to him."

"No way!" I said.

"C'mon," she said as she grabbed my hand to walk with her.

"Noooo!" I was mortified.

"Jeremy, have you met my friend Natasha? She's a junior."

There I stood, like a deer in headlights. I couldn't believe Cathy put me on the spot like that.

He looked at me, and gave me the cutest smile. "Hey, Natasha, very nice to meet you."

"Hi." I felt stupid. It was the only word that could come out of my mouth. It was like the cat really had my tongue.

The next thing I knew, Jeremy and I were engaged in really good conversation. I thought to myself, *Wow, this guy really likes me. He's really interested in what I have to say.*

It was too good to be true. An hour of talking and playing the drinking game went by. I never knew what it felt like to be drunk. The room spun. I laughed and laughed at pretty much everything. My heart raced and my stomach churned. My vision became a little blurred. I could hear Jeremy and his football buddies laughing and chanting. I heard another voice from a distance say, "Jeremy, she's hot! Are you gonna get a piece of that?" I could hear other things being said, but at that moment the voices just echoed in my head.

I don't know how much time had gone by, but I felt constricted, almost like a ton of bricks had been placed on my chest. I could barely get my eyes opened. But as I cracked them open slightly, I saw foggy shadows above me.

"Oh no!" I screamed.

Confusion sat in and I had been in somewhat of a paralyzed state.

I could see Jeremy and a few of the other guys. I wondered what they were doing. I looked to my right and saw a door closed. I realized I was in one of the bedrooms upstairs. But I didn't see Cathy anywhere. In fact, I didn't see any of the other girls who were at the party.

I tried to cry out for her, but the words could barely slip out of my mouth. The word no was the only one I could spit out.

And there I went. I slipped into that dark, dead, and isolated garden again. There I lie in that dirty, muddy ditch. Instead of the monster that haunted me for years, these were new and different monsters. They were more hideous and evil than I've ever encountered. I let out bloodcurdling screams. One of the monsters said, "Shut up! Shut your mouth!" Simultaneously, I felt a hand press hard against my mouth. Not even a muffled sound could be made. The other revolting monster held both my arms down above my head as he stood behind me.

In my mind, I cried out for God. I asked him, *Why me!? Why have you left me alone, again?*

If I wasn't sure before then, I was so sure at that very moment that God had been upset with me. God had abandoned me.

I lie in that garden naked and ashamed. I had been clothed with indignity, humiliation, mortification, and torture. The monsters laughed and mocked me. The agony and pain had been continually inflicted on my body.

I screamed inside, *Stop! Please stop!* I felt my flesh being torn apart.

I saw the fangs of one monster above me as his saliva dripped on my face. I turned my head to the left with my eyes shut tight, because his malevolent appearance scared me half to death. My soul's existence in this desolate garden couldn't take it anymore; it slipped into a black hole. All of my awareness and consciousness had slipped into a coma-like state, and all went black.

## CHAPTER EIGHT

# DAMAGED GOODS

JOB 13:15:

Though he slay me, yet will I hope in him; I will surely defend my ways to his face.

My head felt like it had been smashed against a brick wall. It just pounded and pounded. It was like my head was being bashed open. My eyes opened up to an overly bright room. The blinds were opened. I looked down at my body with only my bottoms on and completely bare up top. I curled my body into fetal position and began sobbing uncontrollably. I could hear the emotional pain reflected in the sounds of my anguish.

Cathy walked in. "Natasha! What's the matter? You need to get dressed. Last night you were out of control," she said in her cocky tone.

"Cathy, what are you talking about? What happened to me? And where were you?"

"Girl, you were all over Jeremy. There were so many people here. He just said you guys were going upstairs for some privacy."

"First of all, I don't remember even so much as giving him a kiss. And privacy!? Is that what he told you?" I cried.

"Why are you so upset?" she asked. "You two looked like you were having a great time."

I kept sobbing, though. "Cathy, I think…umm…"

"You think what?" Cathy asked, annoyed.

"That he attacked me, him and his other friends!"

"What!? Okay, you need to clear your head. No way! Jeremy wouldn't do that," she said, upset. "In fact, it was probably a mistake even inviting you here. Everybody hooks up, Natasha. That's what happens in high school. You can't go around accusing people just because you feel guilty for being loose," she added so coldly.

"What? Do you think I'm lying? I trusted you. I thought you were my friend?"

"It's almost ten o'clock. Your Dad should be here soon. He called you about half hour ago. I told him you were washing up. And by the way, it's probably a good idea we don't hang out anymore. My reputation in school is everything. And word of advice: grow up, Natasha."

As I sat up slowly, it was as if my head weighed like a ton of bricks. I took a gander at the inside of my thighs because they ached so much. There were ugly bruises. I thought, *Mom and Dad can never find out about this. They would kill me.*

Dad finally arrived and waited in the car for me. I walked out without saying good-bye to Cathy. My heart hurt, my soul hurt, my body hurt. The pain I'd been suffering for years had only now deepened. How could I go on after this? It was torture sitting through the sermon at church. The topic was "trusting God even when you don't understand it." I started to think more and more. How could I trust or understand God's reasoning for allowing me to keep going through this? I paid no attention to the pastor. I had tuned him out completely. After, I took two Valium pills as soon as I got home and just passed out. My mind tumbled back into that other world that coexisted with my real world. I dreamed I was running through that beautiful, vibrant garden, when all of a sudden, I heard a loud roar. I looked back and saw an abnormally enormous lion, a giant. He chased me, trying to catch me so that his teeth could shred me to pieces. I ran and I ran as the lion's roars became louder and louder. I could sense he was very close to me. Then the light-brown lion's appearance changed. He had transformed himself into a half lion, half some kind of other beast with long, muscular, humanlike legs. Fear seeped through my pores like sweat. I tried screaming, but just like in my past nightmares the screams had been silent. I had run so fast and so far that I wound up in that black, dead garden again. I couldn't see anything in front of me or behind me. It was pitch black. But I could hear the sound of terror still chasing me. Now I screamed again.

"Tasha! Tasha, Honey, its Mom." Mom woke me up.

My eyes opened and I was short of breath. I sat up and could see Mom right there, sitting beside me on my bed. I hugged her really tightly. "I love you, Mom." I squeezed her some more.

"Love, what is the matter? Please talk to me," Mom said desperately with watery eyes. "I thought you were turning the corner. You just stayed over a friend's house. Is there anything you want to tell me?"

Oh, there was so much I had to tell her, but I just couldn't. It had already gotten way too out of control. I'd allowed myself to be defiled over and over again. I thought about the night at Cathy's house. I felt guilt. I blamed myself. I allowed this to happen to me. If I told her or anyone else, they'd think I was lying because I believed that I'd brought it upon myself. Besides, my innocence had been stripped away from me a long time ago. What difference did it make at that point? I've grown into this curvy, tiny-waisted, and well-endowed young lady. Even though I wore T-shirts and sweats to hide my body, it was almost as if the boys had x-ray vision like Superman. The beauty that everyone saw in me, I had considered to be a curse. I didn't want to be pretty. Pretty had gotten me nothing but heartache and pain. Now I would be labeled with vile words, a young lady who was thought to be promiscuous. Even though that had been far from the truth, this had to be yet another ugly secret I would have to keep to myself.

"I'm okay, Mom. I just had a nightmare."

"Was it that garden nightmare again, Sweetheart?" Mom asked.

"Ah…, no. I actually don't remember. It's okay. Right at this very moment, I feel safe here with you," I answered while my head laid on her chest. Tears just flowed.

"I'm going to make an appointment for you to talk with someone again. I can't help you, Sweetheart, if you don't talk with me." Mom just began crying. "I won't stop praying to the Lord for you. God loves you, Honey, and so do I."

*God loves me? Really? Did she just say that?* I thought.

How can God love someone but not save them?

The more I thought about it, the angrier I got.

I couldn't express even my anger to her, because she'd wonder why and become suspicious. My heart had then given birth to all of those feelings of anger, resentment, and bitterness. I learned to bottle up every single emotion inside. My heart turned into stone.

The weeks following that horrific night were a residual reminder of it. I thought it had been swept under the rug, but not quite. In the hallways at school other students would walk by me, and with the endless whispering, they'd say things like, "That's her. That's the girl I was telling you about."

The stares were endless. Some guys would walk by and laugh at me. I couldn't take it anymore. How could it be that I had been the one violated, yet I was the bad guy? I had been shunned by most. The rumor that had been going around at my high school was that I was "easy." One afternoon, after being mocked, laughed at, spoken badly about, I couldn't take it anymore. For the first time in a long time, I prayed to God:

> *Lord, I know I've been mad at you. I'm sorry for feeling abandoned by you. And I know you hear me. Is it a sin to want to end my life? Since I can't hear you, I would think maybe it might be. But I'm asking you to forgive me ahead of time. Forgive me for being a coward. Forgive me for being so weak. But I just can't live with this pain anymore. It's already too late for me. I'm damaged goods. I'm praying that when I finally do it, you can give me a pass and please let me still make it into heaven. Mom and Dad always told me that in heaven there is no pain, no suffering, and no sickness. Well, God, that's what I want. And please heal Mom and Dad's pain—put it away from their hearts after I'm gone. Even after all of it, thank you, Lord, that you gave me to the best parents ever. Okay, here I go. Please forgive me!*

I opened my locker, slid my hand inside my gym bag, and took out the new bottle of pills I had just purchased earlier that week. I put it inside my pocket. I heard the bell rang. I was going to be late to class. But I wasn't going to class anyway. I went into the bathroom instead. I couldn't wait to do this after school or at home. It was too painful. I became desperate and had to end the pain as soon as possible. I went inside one of the stalls. I sat on the toilet crying. I just started to swallow the pills in small bunches. Before I knew it, I'd swallowed all of them. My life started flashing before my eyes. A flood of memories rushed like

I had been watching a home-movie video. Birthday parties filled with so much love; waking up Christmas mornings to find all of my gifts under the tree. All of the nights Dad would read to me at bedtime, praying together as a family…then the overwhelming memories of horror, the monster's face, and then the faces of the new monsters in my pathetic life. My eyes were crisscrossed. I felt like I was starting to have a heart attack. My stomach screeched with pain as I crouched over. I began sweating profusely. My mouth started foaming. I saw a light, and then I saw nothing at all.

Good-bye, miserable world.

## CHAPTER NINE

# Runaway From Life

Mark 4:40

He said to his disciples, "Why are you so afraid? Do you still have no faith?"

*Where am I?* I heard beautiful songs of birds. I gazed up at the breathtaking, powder-blue skies airbrushed with the floating, cotton-like clouds. My surroundings were so bright, almost blinding. I felt a great sense of peace that I hadn't felt since I was a little girl. I looked at my hands, my arms, and down at my legs; I was four years old again. It was the innocent me, the happy girl who believed in rainbows that are God's promises, and in angels. It was "the happy Natasha." *Did I make it into heaven?* I began walking, and in front of me was the most amazing, decorative garden I had ever seen. This is the garden I dreamed about so long ago. The garden was so full of life. The flowers varied from bright, neon pink and orange peonies; tall, bright, yellow sunflowers; and huge bushels of white and crimson-red roses. The aroma in the garden had been so delightful. Not even the earthly flowers smelled as rich and pure as these.

A voice called out, "Natasha."

"Who is that?" I asked, looking around me.

The voice spoke again. "Natasha, this is your garden."

Instantaneously, I heard a lot of crying and someone praying. I thought, *Wait, that sounds like Mom.*

I heard beeping noises and chaos. There were a few voices talking. They sounded far away and echoed almost as if they were talking inside of a tunnel. I walked a little farther to find out if the voices were coming from inside the garden, but after just a few steps, I fell down spiraling. I passed out.

I awakened again.

There I saw Mom and Dad, then a nurse. *Wait a minute. Am I alive?* My eyes were wide open. The harsh reality then hit me. *Why, God!? Why am I still here? I'm left in this wretched world!* I yelled over and over in my head. I woke up in a hospital with Mom crying over me. Apparently, they had pumped my stomach.

"Oh thank you, Jesus," Mom kept saying. "Thank you for saving my baby's life."

"What are you doing, God!?" I screamed out loud, looking up to the ceiling.

"It's okay, Honey," Mom said, trying to calm me down.

"Noooooo!" I kept screaming. "What do you want from me, God? Why am I still breathing!?" I had become irrational. My soul had been pumped up with so much hopelessness and anger.

Suddenly an alarm rang and a flood of nurses rushed in.

"Mrs. McCarthy, you need to step out," one of the nurses said.

"I'm not leaving her side," Mom argued.

I kept shouting at the top of my lungs. Then I thought, *Great, now they think I'm crazy.*

A nurse rushed up to me with a huge needle in her hand to sedate me.

"NOOOOO!" I yelped. And lights went out again.

I awoke in that heavenly garden again. *What is happening?* I thought.

"Natasha, this is your garden. It still needs a lot of nourishing and I've made you the caretaker of it. There is so much more that will flourish and grow in it. You are needed," the voice said clearly to me.

My eyes cracked opened. Blurry images hovered over me. I worked really hard to open my eyes. The blurred images looked like Mom and Dad. Then as I had been able to focus more, I realized that it was my parents and that I was indeed in that depressing hospital room again.

"Oh, Natasha," Mom cried and put her head on my chest.

"Baby, we are here. We love you so much, Sweetheart," Dad said with tears welling from his eyes as he held my hand.

"What happened?" I asked, a bit confused.

"You're in the hospital, Sweetheart. I want you to just rest. We don't have to talk now," Dad explained.

"Okay, Dad. I don't really want to talk about it anyway. I love you."

After some hours had passed, the doctor on call that night told Mom and Dad that they couldn't stay. After much resistance on Mom's part, Dad had finally been able to convince her to go. Both promised they'd be back first thing in the morning.

I dreaded the fact that I had to eventually face the world again. It had been too cruel. How would I survive? Then I remembered that dream, which felt real. It had been a real garden that I visited between life here on earth and what I believed to be heaven. I knew in my heart it was God's voice that I heard in the garden. I was in awe of Him, even though I couldn't find Him. His voice was clear and close to me. What did He mean by the garden was mine? And why was I needed? I felt a little sense of peace then, knowing I just had to trust Him. It had been the first time that I heard God's voice in my garden. Common sense told me that it didn't make sense, but something extraordinary and audacious told me that I needed to trust God. Our God is audacious. I couldn't shake His presence and that wonderful feeling in the garden. My faith had to be bigger than my fear. I needed to find out what He wanted from me. At that point, I thought, it was going to be a difficult task, but somehow I was still alive and needed to at least try.

A couple of weeks went by. It had been the same routine every day. Mom and Dad came to visit me. Mom had taken a leave of absence from work so she was able to stay most of the day with me. I had mandatory therapy with one of the psychiatrists on staff. But I kept my dark secrets locked up tight inside of me. It didn't make sense to any of the doctors why I would try to take my own life. Here I was, a well-educated, well-spoken girl who came from a good Christian family. Dad was an emergency room doctor and Mom a sergeant in the police department. The doctors began leaning more toward diagnosing me with mental illness. An easy explanation for what didn't make sense. But only God, my monsters, and me knew the truth. I wasn't mentally ill or promiscuous or anything else. I was just a broken girl who had been through some unfair stuff. One night, when Mom and Dad had already gone home, I heard a whisper.

"Pssst. Psst."

Looking to see where it was coming from, I noticed it came from a girl I'd seen only about once or twice before. I thought maybe she was in the same ward I had been in. But I wasn't sure. I kept to myself and didn't want to engage in any conversations with anyone in there.

She was a really pretty girl with dark-brown hair, brown eyes, and an olive complexion.

"Hey," she said.

"Hi."

"You're new here, right?"

"Not really. I've been here a couple weeks already."

"You're so beautiful," she said to me. "What's a girl like you doing in a place like this?"

Lost for words, I said, "Ahh, thanks, but it's kind of a long story. And it doesn't really matter."

"You don't belong in a place like this. I have a way outta here if you're interested."

"Really? How?" I asked skeptically.

"Well, I'm only here voluntarily. I can give you my pass, and at lunchtime it gets crazy busy around, you can walk right outta here."

"I can't do that. My parents have been visiting me every day. And besides, where would I go? My parents would go crazy. I've put them through enough."

The girl gave me a look of doubt. "C'mon, I know why you're here," she said, smiling.

"How do you know why I'm here? You don't even know me."

"Cause I know everything that goes on around here. I know that you tried to kill yourself by overdosing on pills."

"What!? Wait! How do you know that? Who are you?"

"Listen. I'm sorry. I know a beautiful girl like you wouldn't try to take out her own life unless her life was really that bad. Am I right?"

I became confused, but at that same time, I couldn't refute what she said. How could I go back home? How could I return to my secretly dysfunctional life? She was right. Choosing faith or fear became a battle in my mind at that very moment. In one hand, I held on to some hope and faith in God. In the other hand, I held the overwhelming weight of fear that had consumed me for most of my young life. As I prayed in my mind, I caved in to what I was most familiar with. I caved in to the fear. I agreed to escape and run away from my pitiful life.

"So when can we do this?" I asked.

"Atta girl. I have a place. You can stay with me."

"You have your own place? How old are you?"

The girl laughed. "Girl, I'm nineteen."

"How can you afford your own place?"

"You're so cute. Ummm, 'cause I work. I pay my own bills."

I became curious. "Wow. What kind of work?"

"I'll explain what I do later. But for now, we have to make a plan to get you outta here," she whispered."Well, how do you suppose I'm able to leave here without anyone noticing?" I asked her.

"I have an idea. When do your parents usually leave to go home?"

"They're here til visiting hours are over at nine."

"Okay. Here's what you're gonna do. Tomorrow around six or seven in the evening, I want you to pretend you're exhausted and tell your parents you are ready to just call it a night. Insist that you'll see them the next day. That way they'll leave. Only way we can get you outta here is before visiting hours are over. Leave the rest up to me."

"What if they insist on staying?" I asked.She chuckled. "Don't worry. We'll cross that bridge when we get to it. Just do the best you can. Play it off as if you're auditioning for a part in a play."

"All right. I'll try. I hope it works."

"It will. Trust me. I've done this so many times."

I looked at her kind of confused. "Really? Other girls have escaped, too?"

"Yeah, only a couple. But it was a while ago. Now they've slacked on security again. I got you. Don't worry."

So the plan to escape was set. Somehow, I felt a sense of liberation, being freed from my very fractured past. I didn't have to face those monsters again. I apologized to God in my mind. But somehow I knew He wouldn't leave my side.

I closed my eyes to go to sleep. And it seemed like minutes later, I heard birds. I opened my eyes and saw that I had been lying in a bed of roses. The roses were every color of the rainbow. It was beautiful.

The voice said, "Stay, Natasha. I need you to stay."

"Natasha?" There was pause. "Natasha?"

I opened my eyes. The nurse kept calling my name to wake me up. It was breakfast time. God had been chasing me in my dreams. I knew it was His voice commanding me to stay. As soon as the nurse left, I immediately began to pray:

*Lord, thank you for talking to me in my dreams. Thank you for trying to help me. I know you're here with me, but I just can't stay here in this hospital. I can't stay in my current situation. I can't take the chance of being hurt again. I can't take the chance that I would try to hurt myself and my parents again. All I ask of you is that when I take on this journey in my life, that you protect my parents from heartbreak. God, forgive me again, but I just can't stay here.*

After the day had gone by, I kept telling Mom and Dad how much I loved them. I told them as much I could so that they would remember it when I wasn't around anymore. The sun went to bed and evening had finally arrived.

My nerves were rattled. I couldn't believe that I was actually going to do it. I was going to run away from my life and never look back. Lucinda, the girl who was going to save me, had been so cool and calm about the whole thing. Thinking back to that time is a fog. All I know is that the next thing I knew, I had entered the place where Lucinda said she lived. She forgot one very important detail to mention: she lived in a motel. And it wasn't just a motel; it was seedy and in the worst part of town. I had a really bad feeling. I thought, *What have I gotten myself into?*

## CHAPTER TEN

# TRAFFICKED

JOB 3:11–16

Why did I not perish at birth, and die as I came from the womb?

Why were there knees to receive me and breasts that I might be nursed?

For now I would be lying down in peace; I would be asleep and at rest with kings and rulers of the earth, who built for themselves places now lying in ruins,with princes who had gold, who filled their houses with silver.

Or why was I not hidden away in the ground like a stillborn child, like an infant who never saw the light of day?

The evening sky became quiet and still. The vault of heaven had been embellished with bunches of twinkling, bright stars. I imagined it reflected the new peace that would chase me down. Oh how wrong I was. Lucinda and I entered her *"apartment."* But it hadn't been an apartment at all; it was more like a suite in a cheap motel. The tiny kitchen was the loneliest room in the apartment. The small area that looked like a living room had a full-size bed toward the back, dressed with a dated floral bedding sheet.

Immediately, I asked, "Why are we at a motel?"

"Don't worry, Natasha," Lucinda replied. "This is where I live for now. It's convenient and affordable for me."

Somehow, I sensed deep down inside she wasn't being completely forthcoming with me. But at the time, naive sixteen-year-old Natasha wanted to believe her. So I did.

I heard water running from inside of the bathroom. I looked over and became startled when a man walked out. I gasped and looked over at Lucinda.

She gave me a calculated look.

"Who is that?" I asked.

"So you are, Natasha?" the man asked as if he were expecting me.

He scared me. He was a big, bald, muscular guy. He wore a guinea white T-shirt, and a big gold chain with a big cross that dangled from it; he had big tattoos on his forearms. My heart pounced in my chest.

"Lucinda?" I looked at her shrugging my shoulders.

"Oh, where are my manners? My name is Kage. Lucinda, you weren't kidding. She's a beauty."

Lucinda stood in the corner by the door, wearing a deviant smile on her face.

"Lucinda, what's going on? You promised me I'd be safe."

"Natasha, you are safe. Kage takes good care of me. And he's gonna take good care of you, too," she said.

"I changed my mind. I want to go back," I said as I started to walk toward the door.

Kage stood in front of me and then grabbed both of my upper arms.

I told him, "Let go of me!"

"You're not going anywhere, Sweetheart. We can do this the hard way or the easy way. If you don't calm down, I'm gonna make you calm down. You decide."

But I continued to resist him. Before I knew it, he punched me right on my head. The room spun. It looked like Kage had a needle in his hand. I felt debilitated and just couldn't move, and then suddenly, I felt a sharp sting on my arm.

I awoke again in that garden of despair. All of the plants and flowers around me were dried up and dead. I began sinking in quicksand. My head bobbed all the way back, trying to catch a breath. I could hear a bone-chilling voice. I looked up and realized I remained in that prison of a room again. My arms were tied up. My vision was dim. *Who is that?* I thought. I didn't recognize who this stranger was. He appeared older, with salt-pepper hair. He was about in his early forties. He began rubbing my head. I couldn't scream. I screamed in my head. The monster's face started to laugh as he overpowered me. The pain he continually inflicted on me became a numbness after a while. A short time had passed. Another monster entered the room as my limp body laid there. He intruded upon me, savoring me in his nauseating desire. *Do these monsters know that I am only sixteen? Why didn't I listen? I shouldn't have left.* Thoughts continued to flood my mind. Before I knew it, I didn't know how long I had been strapped to that bed, but it seemed like forever. Monster after monster continued to relentlessly invade me. I didn't know if it had been hours, days, or weeks that passed by. All I knew was that it just kept going. The sun shone, and soon after, nights arrived. Day after day, the suffering continued. My mouth was parched with thirst. My belly ached from hunger. The only thing I could do was pray out loud.

One of the monsters became irritated with my praying. "Shut your trap!" He punched me and I lost all consciousness.

Loud fire truck sirens sounded from outside. My head felt like someone hit it with a sledgehammer. My eyes struggled to open. I could only see through one eye. The sun peeked in through the dreary floral curtains. I looked around. The monsters were all gone. I tugged on my right arm as hard as I could with what little energy I had left. They were tied onto the bed with some kind of fabric.

"God, please!" I yelled. "Please let me get these off of me! Help me, God!"

Tugging and pulling as hard as I could, my left hand somehow slipped through the looped tie. I reached over to untie my right hand. Weakness had a hold on me as I tried getting up from the bed, but all I could do was roll off it. The ground was filled with filth, and there I was as I wriggled myself across the floor toward the door. Once making it to the door, I reached up to grab the knob to help myself up. My body trembled with fear. When I had finally been able to open it, I ran out into the street and hastened as fast as I could. As I ran, I heard a loud honking noise and I looked to my left. The car screeched and came to a stop just inches away from hitting me. I had fallen to the ground in slow motion in my mind. I thought, *God, save me!*

Voices echoed.

"Are you okay? Are you okay?" There was a pause. "Hi, please send an ambulance right away! I found a young girl… Yes. She looks like she's been beaten up pretty bad… I don't know. She's maybe about fifteen or sixteen years old. Please hurry."

The woman spoke on a public pay phone, just a short distance from me. Although my eyes were closed, I could hear her cry for help.

Sirens pierced my ears. Police and medics surrounded my near-lifeless body. *Am I having a nightmare? Where am I?* Disoriented thoughts swarmed me.

I could faintly hear from a short distance someone saying, "Oh, my God, this is the girl. Natasha McCarthy. She's been missing for almost three weeks. It's been all over the news."

I heard another voice say, "It's a miracle. She was thought to be dead."

*Dead? Missing for three weeks?* I asked myself.

The horror that took place the last three weeks started to rewind in my mind. If I could remember correctly, there were over forty monsters that I came in contact with. My belly suddenly felt sickened.

"She's been badly beaten."

I continued hearing different voices speaking as I was carefully lifted up from the ground onto a stretcher and into an ambulance.

Oxygen. Oh wonderful oxygen as they placed the mask on me. An IV had been inserted, too. I had been dangerously dehydrated. The voices became more and more faint. They sounded far away. Then there was no sound at all.

## CHAPTER ELEVEN

# A Tree of Life

Proverbs 13:12

Hope deferred makes the heart sick, but a longing fulfilled is a tree of life.

The fragrances all around me were overwhelming. Pink skies, purple clouds, and dazzling butterflies decorated the atmosphere. My feet walked on plush grass, which felt more like I had been walking on goose-feathered pillows. Perfectly trimmed bushes, each one a different color, were landscaped across a curvy pathway. The air was crisp and fresh. There were tall, warm sunflowers ahead of me again. They were eye-popping. The field was endless. Sunflowers were everywhere. I ran right through them with my arms spread out. The sensation was like pure silk on my fingers. Surely, I had to be in heaven. Laughter filled my belly. Happiness found me again. From a far distance, I could see the most remarkable tree. A tree that I don't think even ever existed on the earth or the creation of it. I kept running toward it. It was magnetic and its presence kept pulling me closer toward it. My eyes were completely fixed on this tree. The closer I got, the bigger and taller it appeared. Something familiar was before me. It had been that bed of roses where each rose had been a different color, like a rainbow. Then I noticed the tree again. It had been like a morphed, supernatural tree. It resembled a beautiful southern magnolia tree, about eighty feet tall. The magnolias were the color of flawless ivory. The trunk of this tree reminded me of a palm tree. But in this wondrous tree were all kinds of fruit. In it were cherry-red apples, and lime-green apples, too. The yellowest of lemons and fuzzy, giant peaches were there, as well. Dark, sizeable cherries and figs dangled like jewels off its branches. Amazing! Plums, pears, and bright, plump oranges resided with each other on this divine tree, too. The leaves, emerald in color, were each shaped differently. Its leaves had to be about ten to twelve inches long. They waved at the fresh air. A tree like this doesn't exist. For on earth, each of these fruits grew separately on its own kind of tree, but not this one. Light radiated all around it. My eyes were mesmerized.

*What kind of tree is this?* I asked myself.

"Natasha," His voice spoke.

I knew it was Him. The hairs on the back of my neck stood up from amazement.

"Natasha."

"I hear you, but I can't see you," I called out as I looked all around me.

"Natasha, do you want to know what kind of tree this is?"

"Yes, I do want to know what kind of tree it is. It's beautiful. I've never seen such a tree, not even in fairy-tale storybooks."

"Natasha, this is the 'Natasha Tree,'" His voice said.

"Huh? I don't understand."

"This is a tree of life. This tree is you."

Tears welled up in my bright green eyes. I couldn't stop crying.

"Natasha, why do you cry?"

"God, I know you know the answer to that question. But I know you're probably asking because you want to hear me say it. So I will… I'm crying because you say I'm that tree. But that tree is not only unique, but it's out of this world. It's colorful, beautiful, and full of life. That is definitely not me. I hate my life. I'm no good. My presence is dark and gloomy. I've lost all hope," I replied through my tears.

I fell to my knees, my head bent down in shame. How could it be that I'm weeping in the middle of this perfect, safe place?

I couldn't see Him, but it was as if someone had embraced me, hugging me tightly.

"Natasha, this tree is you."

"I'm sorry to challenge you, God. But this tree is so not me."

His voice said again, "Let me show you what this tree has been through."

It had been like a series of quick, clear images flashing before me. Starting with a tiny seed in pitch blackness as it had been planted deep down in the soil. The darkness lasted what seemed like an eternity. Time crept slowly as the buds finally began to sprout. The tree began growing quickly. In the process of its growth, images of torrential downpours came upon it. A series of hurricanes, floods, and tornados pummeled this tree, but there it stood with its roots planted firmly into the ground. Winds whipped the tree. Its bark was peeling and falling off. The bark had taken a pretty good beating. Its trunk bent all the way to the right, then to the left. It arched forward and backward. The elasticity of this tree was inexplicable. This tree would just not break. Even lightning struck the tree. Branches violently broke off it. But there it still stood, regal and tall. As the black, thick clouds passed and the skies finally opened up, the sun showed its face again. The sun ruled the blue skies once more and there were no more clouds. After weathering the storm, this phenomenal tree defied all of the laws of nature. Its branches began to grow again. The tree produced every kind of fruit on its branches. God's handiwork was perfect. Suddenly, the images stopped.

"Do you see now, Natasha?" His voice asked.

Hope sprung into my soul. Its light around it beamed like no other light I've ever seen. I realized the light was Jesus. The tree and I were connected somehow. Did I really believe I could be like this tree? Had I just been dealt an unfair card in life? Or could it be that I am just like this tree? Hope had given birth in my heart. Could it be, I had a chance for a better life?

"I think so," I answered with a little doubt.

"Natasha. Speak your truth. It will set you free. Remember, this tree is you."

"Speak my truth? What do you mean, God? You know my truth."

"Natasha. Always remember that you are a tree full of life."

"Natasha. Natasha. Can you hear me?" It was Mom's voice.

Then she wept and wept on. I could hear doctors talking with her. They informed her that I fell into a coma. The horrific truth had been revealed to her about my attack in that grim motel. Apparently, there had been a string of girls who had gone missing. And no one really knew at the time too much about it, but it was believed that girls were being taken and sold into prostitution. Whoever heard of this? Somehow, by the grace of God, I had possibly escaped that demise.

"Natasha. It's time," He spoke.

My eyes opened. There stood my beautiful Mom and Dad right next to me.

What was once a dreadful place for me, being in the hospital with my parents at that very moment became my place of refuge. *Thank you, God!*

## CHAPTER TWELVE

# SECRETS

LUKE 12:2–3

> There is nothing concealed that will not be disclosed, or hidden that will not be made known. What you have said in the dark will be heard in the daylight, and what you have whispered in the ear in the inner rooms will be proclaimed from the roofs.

The mirror reflected my bruised and swollen jaw. My eye was purple and completely shut. I felt my wounded cheek and it was painful to the touch. Weird, but I was relieved to see my flawed reflection. It had been proof that I was still alive and breathing. Beyond my fractured image, I could see that healthy, whole, and happy little girl somewhere deep down inside of me. *There is more than this*, I thought. *But what? How do I pick up the broken pieces of my life?* The pieces were tiny bits that couldn't be glued back together again. But I remembered the tree that had been to hell and back. The little spark of hope had lit in me. I wanted that spark to turn into a fire. A fire that burned so deep inside of my soul. To create a passion in me, not only to live, but to let others know that if I could survive the torrential storm, so could they. I wanted to bear fruit just like that tree.

There was a knock on the bathroom door in my hospital room.

"Tasha, Baby. Are you okay in there?"

"I'm okay, Mom. I'll be right out."

I couldn't understand why I went through what I did. And I didn't know what was to come. All I could say in a low whisper under my breath was, "Thank you Jesus." I started to sound like Mom. She was always thanking Jesus under her breath.

Mom was standing right by the door waiting. Without a word said, she embraced me as I held onto the walker. I'd suffered a concussion, a broken rib, my left calf had been fractured; twelve sutures on my upper eye lid and my body felt like it had been run over by a truck.

"Sweetheart, I'm sorry to have to tell you this. I know you've been through so much already. But the police are stopping by soon."

"Police? How come?"

"Well, the detective on your case has a bunch of pictures he wants to show you. They want to know if you recognize anyone from the photos. They want to find who's responsible for doing this to you. And so do Dad and me."

"Aww, Mom. I'm kinda scared."

"I know, Sweetheart. If you're not ready, I can just have them come by another day. It's just the sooner you can help identify who did this, the sooner they can find them."

"Okay, I'll do it. I'll be fine."

"You're so brave. They are bringing a sketch artist, too."

"Where's Dad?" I asked.

"He'll be here soon. This whole situation has been really tough for him."

Mom's eyes were so puffy. I could tell she had cried her eyes out. But I knew she was trying to be strong in front of me.

I couldn't stop thinking if they only knew I'd been dealing with monsters since I was little. I knew I had to keep that a secret from them. I didn't want them to be hurt any more than they'd been hurt already. Besides, Joe had been out of the picture. My family and I hadn't seen or heard from him in years. My slumber had lasted several hours after. My body felt jet-lagged. During that time, detectives had stopped by, but I had been knocked out. Time was of the essence, but they assured they'd be back the following day.

During that time in the late eighties, it was the age of pay telephones. Technology had not been as sophisticated as it is today. There were no surveillance cameras at every corner of the streets or businesses. Cell phones weren't really popular yet, either. And social media didn't even exist yet. So the police had their work cut out for them on finding the perpetrators.

The following day was mayhem. I sat in the recreational room with detectives, looking at a ton of photos, but I didn't see Kage or Lucinda in any of them. I also spent quite some time with the sketch artist, giving him details of Kage and Lucinda. The sketches eerily resembled them.

After a few days had passed, Mom told me I was being transferred to a Christian rehabilitation center. There I would get physical therapy and counseling, too.

A week had gone by. I began feeling like I belonged there. Each of the rooms had a Bible in it. I started reading it every day, beginning with the book of Genesis. And the food they provided there had been pretty good. One day in the cafeteria, a girl sat down next to me. It looked like she might be pregnant. But I wasn't sure.

"Hey." She looked over at me with a smile.

"Hi," I said.

"I'm Mia. What's your name?"

"I'm Natasha. But some people call me Tasha."

"What happened to you?" she asked me.

"What do you mean?"

"Well, aren't we all here for something? I'll start with me if you want."

"Sure."

"First of all, I'm twenty years old. And as you can see, I'm pregnant. I'm only four months, though. The doctors say I'm just retaining a lot of water."

"Congratulations. Are you married?" I asked her.

As she looked down, she said, "No, I'm not. My baby's father has disappeared on me."

"Disappeared?" I asked, confused."Well, yeah. We were so happy. I mean he was so happy, too, that we were having a baby together."

"So what happened?"

"He had a problem with substance abuse. I tried to help him, but over time he just got worse," Mia answered, her eyes tearing up.

"So he just left you?"

"No. I mean, yes. But not the way everyone thinks. You see, we were living together. One night, he decided he was going out. I knew better. I knew he was going out to find his next fix. I told him not to go. But he had become so irrational. And then he never returned back home."

"Do you think maybe he changed his mind about being a daddy? Maybe it was too much pressure for him."

"No. That's not it. I know something is wrong. I called the police that night, but they said there was nothing they could do. They said he's a grown man and probably just left me. Deep down inside I knew it wasn't true. He loved me. And he loved our baby, too. He wouldn't just leave us."

"What about his family? Have you tried reaching out to them?"

"I never met his family. He was very secretive about his past. But told me he didn't have a family, anyway. He said his parents died in a car accident when he was little."

"Oh, my goodness. That's horrible."

"Yeah, I know. I always thought that was one of the reasons he was crazy at times. We were only together for two years before I got pregnant, but I feel like we've been together forever."

"Wow. I'm so sorry. So what are you doing here?" I asked, still confused, thinking what did all of that had to do with her being in a place like this.

"That's just it. I'm kind of ashamed about it. But I tried to take my life. I know it's terrible. I love my baby. And I love Junior. That's his name by the way. They are all I have. I have no one else. I have no other family. How could I raise my baby on my own? I figured I could just end my pain once and for all."

Even though I didn't know Mia and had just met her, I felt compelled to hug her at that moment. I embraced her. She embraced me back as she cried.

"I'm so sorry," I told her. "I know we just met. This may sound weird, but you have me."

"Thank you." She looked at me with grateful eyes.

Thereafter, as the days went by, I began reading stories out of the

Bible to Mia. She didn't believe in God, but she allowed me to read to her. She figured it'd be good for her baby. It had been healing for me, too.

"Mia, I hope you don't mind, but I want to ask you a sensitive question."

"Okay," she said.

"Have you always not believed in God?"

"I've always wanted to. But if there is really a God, why did he allow me to be born to parents who didn't want me? My mother supposedly was a crackhead who gave me up. My dad, well, let's just say I don't even know anything about him. I lived in foster home after foster home. No one loved me enough to want to adopt me. The idea that a God existed had once been in my mind as a kid. But as the years passed, I thought, if there was really a God, He wouldn't allow babies be born into such detrimental circumstances."

"Mia, I agree with you that life just isn't fair. I questioned a lot of things growing up, too. But God is real."

"Ha! That's funny coming from you," she said sarcastically.

"Why is that so funny?"

"Of course, you would believe in God. Why wouldn't you? You grew up in a loving family with both of your parents who raised you and love you. You poor little rich girl. Poor little Tasha."

"Mia, you don't really know that much about me. Do I have loving parents? Yes, I do. Did they provide a great home for me? Yes, to the best of their ability. Was my childhood one that everyone wished they had? Absolutely not! You don't know anything about me, Mia," I said angrily.

Mia judged me. She didn't know about my secret. She only knew about my horrific encounter with Kage and Lucinda. But she didn't know about the monsters of my past. She didn't know about the dead garden I had been living in for most of my life.

"I'm sorry, Tasha. What I meant is, yes, I'm sure you've had your problems. Doesn't everyone? But your little problems are nothing compared to mine. I'm just saying. I guess if there is a God, He probably has His favorites. I'm certainly not one of His. You know what I mean?"

"No, Mia, I don't know what you mean. But I'll tell you this. I have a big secret. It's secret that only me, one other person, and God know about. And it's a very ugly, painful secret."

"Oh? Do you want to talk about it?"

"No, I can't and I won't. Listen, I can't force you to want to sit with me and read the Bible. And I'm not going to try and convince you that God is real. All I want you to know is that I'm here for you if you need me."

"Thank you, Tasha. I'm sorry. I hope I didn't upset you and I appreciate all of your help. I'd like to continue hearing stories out of the book. What else can I do while I'm in here anyway? And I guess it can't hurt, right?" She chuckled.

Mia's unbelief suddenly became a challenge for me. In some weird way, I felt like I was getting closer to Him. Then I remembered when He spoke to me in the garden, and told me to speak my truth.

I wondered if he meant to speak my truth to Mia—or to anyone else, for that matter. But I just couldn't. Shame weighed heavily on me. The monster in the garden needed to be kept secret always.

## CHAPTER THIRTEEN

# CHAINED

EPHESIANS 6:12

> For our struggle is not against flesh and blood, but against the rulers, against the authorities, against the powers of this dark world and against the spiritual forces of evil in the heavenly realms.

The high winds screamed and howled as the thunder rattled the windowpanes. The barbed lightning continued to shoot out of the sky. It was seven o'clock in the morning, but it looked more like early evening. The sky had been somber. It reflected the way I felt at the moment. Why was I so ungrateful? My heart was still beating and I had breath in my lungs, but sadness continued to creep in. I learned little by little to pray each time that happened to me. The monsters of my past still taunted me. The detective was stopping by that day to meet with my parents and me. I started to regain more strength in my legs. Physical therapy was helping me a lot. The counseling didn't help so much. But when I read the Bible, it did help me. I'd also somewhat become Mia's spiritual counselor, too. Go figure. A damaged girl with a crushed self-esteem was counseling another broken girl. Somehow, it kept me going, even though I battled with keeping the dark secret from my past locked up. I dreamed about it in my sleep. I'd wake up in the mornings thinking about it, and I'd go to bed with the unspeakable memories trapped in my mind. I had become two different girls. One girl who was struggling to believe her true identity of who she really was in Christ, and the other girl who believed she was worth nothing. I had become a prisoner of my past. My mind and spirit had been bound in the chains of fear and shame. I was too young to understand at the time that the devil had a stronghold on me. I hadn't yet grasped the realization that what the devil was really after was my faith. He took pleasure in the state of mind I lived in. But I kept replaying in my head the words that were spoken to me in the garden. God's words: "Natasha, speak your truth." I tried reconciling with those words. I wanted to break free. I wanted to break out of that cocoon of secrets. I wanted the secret to be set free like a beautiful butterfly.

Then they finally showed up. Mom and Dad walked into my room with the detective. The look on Mom's face worried me.

"Hi, Sweetheart," Dad said as Mom hugged me. "Detective Fitz is here to talk with us."

"Hi Natasha," Detective Fitz said. He wore a grey suit jacket, button-down white shirt, and grey slacks.

"Hi," I replied.

"We have some good news, but I need to ask you some more questions."

I looked over at Mom and Dad, then him. "Okay," I said.

"The good news is that we had a couple of witnesses come forward. One of the witnesses said on the same day you escaped, they saw two men and one young woman earlier that morning that left the room where they held you captive. One of the men and the young woman she described matched the composite sketch. You mentioned a bunch of other men, too. I know you said you don't remember what they looked like. But was there another man with Kage the day you were abducted?"

"No. The day I left with Lucinda and met Kage, he was the only man there."

"Natasha, I have a composite sketch of the other man that the witness saw with Kage and Lucinda. Is it okay if I show you? I just want to know if he looks familiar." He took out a big piece of paper out of his brown envelope folder.

I looked at the sketch. The hairs on the back of my neck stood up. But why? I didn't know who this man was. He frightened me. The words were stuck in my mouth.

"Sweetheart?" Mom said. "What's the matter? Do you recognize him?"

"No. I don't recognize him. It's strange, but he does look familiar to me," I said, trembling. "I don't remember him being one of the men who attacked me. But then again, everything from that time seems like a blur."

"We think these two men are working together. It's believed they are trafficking young girls into prostitution. And the young female who's working with them is what we call their recruiter," the detective explained to my parents.

"Oh, my goodness. What makes you think that?" Mom asked him.

"Well, the witnesses that came forward said that these two men and young woman had been staying at this motel for at least three months. They've been seen with other young women."

"What? Are you kidding me? How come no one called the police?" Dad fumed.

"Well, that's just it," the detective replied. "There was never any disturbance or anyone seen hurt or distressed. After all, it is a motel. They see all kinds of people check in and out all the time. We also checked with the manager and the room was being rented under a husband and wife name. It's obvious the names Kage and Lucinda are not their real names. One puzzling question we have is, why did they let Natasha go? Why she was left behind? It's a mystery. But thank God she was. Mr. and Mrs. McCarthy, she's very lucky to be alive."

"I want those animals found," Dad said furiously. "I won't rest until they are found and arrested."

"We are doing our best, Mr. McCarthy. I give you my word I personally will do everything to find who did this to Natasha," Detective Fitz promised.

"Thank you so much," Mom said to him.

I started to see bits and glimpses of those long days and nights in that room of torture. And all I could remember were images of figures. But it was as if none of them had faces. I just couldn't focus. I had been in and out of consciousness the entire time. It frustrated me that I just couldn't remember.

"Natasha, you've done good. You're a very brave girl. If it weren't for the detailed descriptions that you gave of Kage and Lucinda, we wouldn't have these other witnesses," the detective said. "Mr. and Mrs. McCarthy, I will be in touch. And, Natasha, if you remember anything else, please let your parents know so they can call me, okay?"

"Yes, I will," I promised.

After spending most of the day with Mom and Dad, I couldn't wait to sit with Mia. She and I were bonding. I didn't have siblings. I began feeling like she was the sister I never had. She'd also mentioned that she needed to tell me something important. I wondered what it could've been.

## CHAPTER FOURTEEN

# SILENCE ISN'T GOLDEN

JOSHUA 1:9

"Have I not commanded you? Be strong and courageous. Do not be afraid; do not be discouraged, for the Lord your God will be with you wherever you go."

"What's her name?"

"Natasha. I did good, right boss?'

"Where did you find this one again?"

"She was one of the girls I found at the hospital."

"We gotta get outta here."

"I'm sorry. You said to find girls that looked like her. You said—"

"I know what I said!" yelled the man. "I told you to bring me pictures first! Didn't I?"

"Ahh…"

"Didn't I?"

"Yes, you did. I'm sorry. I just figured she was exactly what you were looking for."

"We need to get out here, now!"

"Wait, what about Natasha?"

"We leave her behind."

"But…"

"But nothing! Let's get out of here now!"

My eyes opened. I sat up quickly. I wasn't sure if I'd just dreamed the whole thing or if it were a memory that surfaced. It was confusing. I could hear the voices, but see no faces. The man's voice definitely wasn't Kage's voice. How could I forget his voice? It was deep and eerie. I'd recognize his voice anywhere. Was there really another man with Kage and Lucinda? If so, I definitely didn't see him or meet him.

"Hey." It was Mia; she startled me.

"Oh hi," I said. "How long were you standing there?"

"Only about a minute. I didn't want to wake you. I can come back, if you want."

"No, no. Come in. Hey, I was thinking of reading the book of John today. What do you think?"

"It really doesn't make a difference to me," Mia said with a concerned look on her face.

"What's the matter, Mia?" I asked.

"Ahh, nothing."

"I can tell something is wrong."

"Ah. It's just today is one of those days."

"Talk to me."

"I'm worried about what kind of mom I'm going to be. I didn't grow up with a mom myself. None of my foster parents really cared about me."

"You're going to be a good mom. You're gonna be good because you are going to give your baby everything you didn't get."

"I haven't given up finding Junior, either. I can't understand why he would take off on us."

"I know it's hard, Mia. But you have to try to focus on getting healthy for you and your baby."

"How can I protect my baby?" Mia said worriedly.

"What do you mean Mia?" I asked.

"Well…um." The words got stuck in her mouth. As I looked on, she looked hesitant to speak.

"What is it?" I asked her again.

Mia began crying. I walked over to her and she cried on my shoulder. I rubbed her back, trying to console her.

"I had a foster dad who hurt me when I was young," she said.

"Oh no. I'm sorry, Mia. How did he hurt you?" I asked.

"It's really hard to talk about it."

"You don't have to tell me. I'm here for you when you need me or ready to talk."

Mia sobbed as I hugged her again, and then she said, "He took away my innocence. I never told anyone because he said no one would believe me anyway." She continued to cry. "And what did it matter if I did tell someone? The damage was already done."

I felt a sickening feeling in the pit of my stomach. I battled at that very moment whether or not to speak my truth to her. What were the chances that she went through the same thing I did? This was my chance to really help her. But I couldn't muster up the courage to share my story with her. Fear had me chained to my secret. Suddenly, my tears couldn't be held back as I cried with her. She had visited that dark and lifeless garden, too.

"Aww, look what I've done. I'm older than you and should be trying to help you instead of you helping me," Mia said through her sobs.

"No, please. It's okay, Mia. I know this is gonna sound weird. But you are helping me," I said to her.

"I hope the God that you believe in helps me to protect my baby the best way that I can," Mia replied. "I'll never leave my baby alone with anyone. Except you, Natasha. I trust you. I never thought I'd say that to any living soul."

"God will protect you and your baby. Thank you for trusting me."

"How do you suppose your God will protect us? He didn't protect me."I didn't know how to answer that question. I had struggled in the past with that question, too. "Mia, I believe that there are going to be some things in life we won't know the answers to. What I can tell you is that I believe that you're alive for a purpose. And now you've been given the gift of carrying life, too."

"I'm scared, Natasha."

"Mia, you're safe here and so is your baby. You just do all you can to be the best mom you can be." I felt silly saying those words to her. I just didn't know what else I could say. I myself felt a little scared. The difference was I believed God was with me. But she didn't believe at all.

"What am I going to do without Junior? What if I never find him? What if something terrible has happened to him? This just isn't fair." Mia just cried hopelessly. All I could do was hold her.

The day quickly went. I'd spent pretty much the whole day with Mia. I read to her. I prayed for her. Once I had been finally back in my room, the wheels wouldn't stop turning in my head. I felt like a big hypocrite. How could Mia trust someone who couldn't even share her own testimony with her? In one sense, I had been too afraid. In the other, I felt that if I opened up about myself to her, she wouldn't be able to get closer to God. She would think that maybe there was no hope. I couldn't take the chance of being responsible for making her feel worse than she already did. I felt I was in over my head with all of this. Immediately, I prayed:

*Lord, I'm so sorry. You told me to speak my truth. I wasn't there for Mia the way that she needed me. Forgive me. Please give me the strength and the courage to speak my truth. If anyone needs to hear it, it is Mia. Please help me Lord. Is that what you meant when you said for me to speak my truth?*

## CHAPTER FIFTEEN

# TRUTH BE TOLD

PSALM 147:3

He heals the brokenhearted
and binds up their wounds.

The ebony sky was bare. Not one star lived in it. I could hear the crickets singing. My body felt displaced. I looked all around me. The air was brisk. I felt a painful chill in my bones. My body had been all muddy. I lie in that dirty ditch in the garden.

I thought, *Please, don't let it be so.*

Had I been trapped in a nightmare for most of my life? I sat up and looked down, and there next to me was a pond. My eyes worked very hard to focus. I saw her reflection. I became frightened. It was a four-year-old little girl. But the four-year-old little girl wasn't me. Somehow she looked very familiar, though. But I felt my physical self, looking into the pond. Bewildering thoughts consumed me. How could that not be me? *Who is the little girl that I see?* Suddenly, a load roar sounded; I recognized who it was. It had been the monster who had taken me that fateful night in the camp log cabin. He began chasing me as he always did. I bolted as quickly as I could. I came across a massive cornfield. The cornstalks appeared like giants to me. I tried to catch my breath as I ran through the maze of corn. I heard the monster call out her name. I tried listening carefully as I ran for dear life. All I could hear, faintly, was her name, and then I heard, "You're such a pretty flower."

Oh, my goodness! I knew that voice. It was my monster. But I couldn't hear the name he called.He called her again and said, "You're such a pretty flower."

I shouted, "You don't scare me anymore. Do you hear me?" I continued to shout. "I'm not alone in this garden with you."

The monster just laughed. His laughter became harder. His voice became deeper. I couldn't see where he was. But I saw the dry soil where there once were streams of spring water. The flowers were not flowers at all. They were desiccated and frazzled. I thought if I had just touched them, they would come back to life. But as my fingers slightly made contact, they fell to the floor like crumbs.

The monster's voice became louder. He kept calling the girl's name. Why couldn't I hear her name?

My legs couldn't run anymore, until I realized I had made it out of the cornfield and into acres of bright-green land. In the middle of this enormous fertile field, I spotted a small cottage. It was beautiful. I had never seen such a place as this one. It was quaint and cozy in size. Alongside of its walls were vines with sumptuous flowers. The flowers were just as divine as the ones I had seen in God's garden. Surrounding the cottage were patches of bright pink daisies. I heard crying. It was the little girl crying. I walked faster to find her. Behind the beautiful cottage was an attached outhouse. As I walked closer to it, I could hear the crying becoming louder. I opened the door slowly. I heard voices coming from the inside. I walked in and stepped into a different dimension. I was in an apartment. There was the little girl I just saw in the reflection of the pond. In a flash I heard,"Mia, you're such a pretty flower."

I looked at the little girl. It *was* Mia! I ran toward her to grab her and take her out of there quickly. But as soon as I could get my hands to reach for her, all of what I had just seen moments ago were gone. There I stood in front of that extraordinary cottage.He spoke. "Natasha, speak your truth."

"Tasha… Tasha, Honey?"

"Mom?"

"What's the matter, Sweetheart? You were talking in your sleep."

"Sleep?" I asked.

"Yes, you just said, 'I can't do it, I just can't.'" Mom replied. "What were you dreaming about, Honey?"

"I don't remember, Mom. I'm fine."

But in my mind, I wondered if my dream meant anything significant, other than feeling guilty for not opening up to Mia. It felt so real. It was definitely God's voice. Why was the familiar monster in my dream? I realized what needed to be done. I needed to tell Mia that I was like her. I needed her to know that she wasn't alone in that lonely, painful, and dark garden. Today was going to be the day I share my secret. It wasn't mine to keep. Mia needed to know about my monster, too.

After spending a nice day with my parents during visitation, I couldn't wait to meet with Mia.Mia's door was closed. I knocked.

"Come in," she said.Mia was sitting in a chair in her room. I was in shock.

"Mia, is that what I think it is?" I said to her.She held a book in her hand. She appeared to be really reading it. "Are you shocked to see me holding a Bible?" She smiled at me.

"Mia, is this for real? Or are you just trying to prank me?" I kind of laughed.

"The strangest thing happened to me early this morning. I just had a strong urge, almost like a curiosity to hold it in my hand. I opened it up and just started reading."

"And? What do you think?"

"Well, I think I'm intrigued. I was a little spooked to read that a snake kind of tricked these two people. It made me want to keep reading. I know you've read to me. But I'm going to admit, I wasn't really paying attention. I figured to reread it myself."

"Wow, Mia. I'm so proud of you," I told her. "Mia, I have to talk to you."

"Uh-oh. What is it? Is it Junior? Did you hear any news about him?"

"Junior? No, silly."

"Of course. I'm sorry. I just can't stop hoping that someone will find out something soon. So what is it?"

"Do you remember when you opened up to me about what had happened to you as a child?"

"Yes. You're the only one I told that to."

"I kind of figured that. Remember when we had a whole conversation about God, and your reasons for not believing in Him? Well, I am just like you, Mia."

"What are you talking about? You are nothing like me, Natasha. First of all, you believe in God. You have the perfect family. You have parents who love you. They chose to have you. They wanted you and they will never leave you. You and I have nothing in common. But I appreciate you trying to help me—"

"Mia, Mia, Mia," I interrupted her rambling. "Mia, let me finish speaking."

"Okay. I'm sorry." She looked at me attentively.

"Mia, you and I are the same. We were both little girls at one time. We both craved safety and refuge. Yes, I grew up with loving parents. But not even my parents could protect me."

"What?" Mia looked confused.

"You see, Mia… I, too, have a monster."

"Monster?" she asked.

"Yes. When I was a little girl, actually four years old, I had been hurt, too. My first cousin who's a lot older than me hurt me."

"Do you mean…?"

"Yes. He stole away my innocence, too. It didn't stop there. He was relentless for five long years."

Disturbance was plastered all over Mia's face as she covered her mouth. She sat up, walked over to me, and hugged me tightly. A rush of relief came over me as I cried hard. I felt a sudden cleansing come over my soul. Mia cried, too.

"Natasha, I would never ever think that you went through anything like me. Oh, my word. You are like me. Thank you! Thank you! Thank you!" She cried some more.

I wondered at this very fragile moment what she had been thanking me about.

"I'm so sorry. Please forgive me for judging you. I'm thanking you for sharing this with me because I always thought something was wrong with me. I thought, throughout all of these years, I didn't deserve to be loved."

As we hugged each other, I felt a warm feeling. I believed that this could be the beginning of healing, not just for me, but for Mia, as well.

"Natasha, your cousin who did that to you is definitely a monster. What ever happened to him?" Mia asked.

"I haven't seen him in years. Oddly enough, my aunt and uncle say they are kind of estranged from him. They don't really say why. And I don't ask because I never want to see him ever again. I've asked God to forgive me, but I've even wished for him to disappear forever."

"What about God? How does he fit into all of this?"

"God has always been with me," I replied. "I know you probably think I'm crazy, but I feel like I was supposed to go through what I did. I should be six feet under, yet here I stand with you. I'm alive. You're alive. We're alive for a reason. You and I tried to take our lives. But we survived. Mia, I wish I knew all of the answers to your questions, but all I have left is my faith. The devil can try to take all else, but I will fight for my faith."

"Wow. I want that, too."

"Mia, can I ask you a big favor?"

"Sure, anything."

"Please do not ever repeat what I just told you. My parents can never find out this. It will break their hearts."

"You have my word, Natasha."

## CHAPTER SIXTEEN

# COMING TO LIGHT

1 JOHN 4:15

This is the confidence we have in approaching God: that if we ask anything according to his will, he hears us.

The sound of the alarm bell filled the halls. The loud commotion a few doors down from me in the rehabilitation center had been disturbing. I stepped out to see what was going on. There were other girls there, too. I didn't see Mia. Immediately, I thought it might have involved her. A troubled girl I'd see quite often wasn't there, either. I could hear one of the other girls crying. The counselor who I grew close to tried assessing the situation. Oh right, my counselor. I haven't mentioned much about her. Everyone called her Ms. Daisha. I always remembered her name because it reminded me of daisies. I guess because part of her name looked like the word daisy. Besides, I also loved daisies, like the ones I'd often imagine in my beautiful imaginary garden. Ms. Daisha kept everything going smoothly at the center. She'd become kind of a role model for me. In the beginning, I hadn't been absorbing the counseling much because my hurts were so deep. But the way she counseled me and the other girls was so nurturing. Let's just say she handled us with lots of tender-loving care. Although she wasn't a teacher, I also learned so much about the stories in the Bible from her. I found out that she was an associate pastor at her church. It made sense that she had a knack for using everyday examples that linked back to God's Word. I had developed a close bond with her. Just as I was about to approach Ms. Daisha to ask what was going on, Detective Fitz walked in with Dad.

*What is he doing here?* I thought. "Is everything okay?" I asked as I hugged Dad.

"Everything is fine, Sweetheart. Detective Fitz is here to show you some more pictures."

"Pictures? Again?" I asked.

"Yes," the detective confirmed. "I know this process isn't easy. But we think we are getting close to finding the people who hurt you."

"Really?" I asked, scared.

"Yes. We have a couple of people of interest. I want to show you these pictures to see if you recognize any of them. Okay?"

"Okay," I said.

Detective Fitz reached into his bag and pulled out mug shots. I looked and looked and looked. Then I gasped.

"What happened?" Dad asked excitedly.

I placed my finger on his picture. I knew who he was.

"Is that Kage, Natasha?" Detective Fitz asked.

I was trembling. "No. But I remember this guy. He's the very first monster I encountered in that hotel room." *How could I forget this monster's face?* I thought. He had salt-pepper hair, and the small mole right above his lip.

"Are you sure?" the detective asked.

"Yes… Yes! I'm positive. I remember that mole, too. It was one of the things I remembered because his smile scared me, and all I could notice was that thing above his lip. Oh! And his hair. I remember his hair being that color, too." I shook as I spoke.

"We are going to bring him in for questioning. But, Mr. McCarthy, would you be willing to bring your daughter to the precinct? We'll have a lineup of more suspects."

I looked at Dad, worried. He returned my gaze, almost like he didn't know how to answer the detective's question. But I made it easy for him.

"Yes, Daddy. Please take me. I want to go. I have to do this," I said while looking at the detective.

"Are you sure, Sweetheart?" Dad asked.

"Yes, I'm positive."

Dad hugged me tightly. "I'm so proud of you, Tasha. You're my brave girl."

"We are going to catch these men and put them away for a long time. I usually don't promise families this, but I promise you, we are going to find them," Detective Fitz said confidently.

"Thank you so much, Detective. God bless you." Dad shook the detective's hand.

Although it made me a little nervous, I felt confident that the detective meant what he said to me. I believed him. I didn't want to worry about not being able to sleep at night. I worried those men would find me and take me away. I knew that if they were caught, they wouldn't be able to hurt me or anyone else ever again. Maybe this was going to be part of the truth that also needed to be told. I read in the Bible that God told Joshua to let us know not to be afraid. I needed to build up my courage.There were loud voices talking in the hall. I overheard about one of the girls trying to hurt herself. She was rushed to the hospital. That must've been the commotion I wondered about earlier. My surroundings were a spiritual battle, I suppose. We were all dealing with some kind of difficulty. But I felt as though I had been getting stronger. Not so much physically. But mentally and spiritually, I was getting stronger. I had adopted a scripture that captured my heart. It was in Philippians 4:13: "I can do all things through Him who gives me strength." I'd whisper it under my breath each time I woke up, and I'd whisper it at night before bedtime.

After our daily group meetings with Ms. Daisha, Mia and I would get together to just talk, to share what we learned.

Later…

"Natasha, I had such a wonderful dream last night," Mia said with a sad smile.

"What was your dream about?" I asked.

"I dreamed that I was in our apartment, the one I lived in with Junior. He woke me up and kissed me on my forehead. He said, 'Mia, I love you and will never leave you again.' It felt so real."

"Aww, Mia. I know that you miss him. Just keep praying. Never stop hoping that he'll come back."

"Well, funny you should say that. Can I tell you something?"

"Sure. What is it?"

"Before I fell asleep last night, I did something that I hadn't done ever in my life."

"What's that?"

"I prayed to God about Junior, and our baby, too," Mia admitted.

"Oh, my goodness!" I exclaimed. "That's great, Mia."

"Yes. And I'm thinking maybe I dreamed about Junior because I prayed for him."

"I'm praying for you, too, Mia."

"After our talk last night, I prayed for you, too, Natasha. You are so strong. I want to be strong like you."

"But, Mia, you are strong. You're stronger than you know," I said. "Do you mind me asking? But how did you and Junior meet anyway?"

It looked like I caught her off guard with my question.

"Oh wow. How did I meet him? It's complicated." Mia looked pensive.

"I'm used to complicated," I said as I laughed.Mia laughed, as well. "I met him at a lounge," she said, embarrassed.

"A lounge? What kind of lounge? I thought you met him when you were eighteen?"

"Well, it was kind of a bar and dance place. I've been around, Natasha. Remember, I didn't have parents like you have. I had a fake identification card. In fact, I still have it. And I do look older than my age." She continued explaining. "He came right up to me. I'm not gonna lie. He intimidated me. He is a lot older too."

"How much older?" I asked.

"He's eight years older than me. So at the time I met him, he was twenty-six years old."

"Oh wow."

"He was with a friend of his. I opened up to him that night and told him pretty much everything about myself. He had a charm about him that made me feel comfortable enough to do that. He offered me a job, too."

"What kind of job?"

"Let's just say I had to keep lonely people company."

I looked perplexed. "Keep people company? Like old people at a home or something?"

"Please don't judge me. It was harmless. I kept guys company. I kept girls company. Junior gave me a place to live. He bought me new clothes and shoes. He saved my life."

"Mia, I still don't understand what kind of job you're talking about," I said, concerned.

"Well, it doesn't matter anyway," she said evasively. "Just trust me when I tell you that Junior was good to me. He is all that I have."

Lord knows all the troubles I've had. I had to take away the judgement glasses off. I couldn't imagine what she was talking about. I didn't know Junior. If he made her happy, I guess that's what mattered. I needed to show her my support. Before going to bed that night, I prayed to God to show her the way. But something deep down inside gnawed at me about her story. It just didn't feel right at all. I needed to dig deeper.

## CHAPTER SEVENTEEN

# THORN IN MY SIDE

2 CORINTHIANS 12:9

But he said to me, "My grace is sufficient for you, for my power is made perfect in weakness." Therefore I will boast all the more gladly about my weaknesses, so that Christ's power may rest on me.

The little girl ran fast across the acres of rich, green land. Her hair was long and black. Then I remembered who the little girl was; it was Mia I had been chasing.

I called out for her while running, yelling, "Mia! It's me, Natasha. Mia! Wait!"

But she wouldn't stop. Behind me I could hear the familiar voice of the enemy. It was my original monster.

Repeatedly, he called out in his sinister voice, "Come here, my Pretty Flowers."

I wondered why he referred to both of us as his flowers. I needed to burst out of this nightmare. "God, please help me! I need to know what's going on," I cried out to the Lord. Somehow I knew God was there, but He was silent.

"Natasha, you're such a pretty flower. I've missed seeing you," the monster said.

I screamed out loud, "Leave me alone! You're not real! You're not really here! What do you want from me?"

"Natasha…? Natasha. It's me, Ms. Daisha."

"Ms. Daisha. Oh, thank God it's you." I hugged her.

"Hey, hey, you're safe, Darling. I came in to check up on you. It's not like you to be late or miss one of our group sessions."

"Oh no. What time is it? Did I miss group?"

"No, Love," Ms. Daisha assured me. "It's only nine fifteen. I was going to have one of the other girls check up on you. But after yesterday's incident, I wanted to come and check on you myself."

"My alarm clock didn't go off. I'm so sorry. I'll get ready quickly and be right there."

"Natasha, I want to tell you that you've come a long way since you've been here. If there's anything you'd like to talk about, you know that I'm here for you."

"Yes, I know. Thank you, Ms. Daisha. I appreciate you."

Ms. Daisha hugged me. "Okay, so I'll see you in a few minutes?"

"Yes." I smiled.

I couldn't wait to meet with Mia later on. I wanted to pick her brain.

The day seemed to whiz by. The group session was really good, too. Ms. Daisha said because of how well I've progressed, they were going to discharge me soon. I didn't want to be discharged. Even though I was happy about how well I had been doing. I felt respected and needed among the other girls there. I felt for the first time in a long time that I had a purpose. Ms. Daisha said it would be about two weeks before I would be released to go home. I didn't know how Mia was going to feel about that. We'd grown a close friendship and I felt like I'd be abandoning her. I needed to tell her first before she found out from someone else.

Early evening arrived...

"Hey, Natasha, guess what?" Mia asked with a bright smile.

"I'm guessing by the look on your face that you prayed again," I said with doubt.

Mia just laughed. "Actually, yes, I did pray again. But that's not what I wanted to tell you."

"Oh, what is it?"

"I had a sonogram done today. I am twenty weeks along and it was just a routine monthly checkup. But the doctor said I could find out the sex of my baby."

"Really!" I said excitedly.

"I'm having a boy!" she screamed happily.

I screamed, too, as we hugged each other tightly. "Oh, Mia, I'm so happy for you. You said you wanted a boy."

"I know. I mean, I'm happy of course that the baby is looking healthy, but I really wanted a boy. Oh, if only Junior were here," Mia said while rubbing her belly.

"Do you have any names in mind?" I asked.

"I have a few in mind but not sure which one to pick."

"I'm so excited for you."

Mia's face quickly changed.

"What's the matter?" I asked her.

"I don't really have anywhere to go," she answered somberly.

"What do you mean?"

"I have no idea where I'm going to live, Natasha. I lost the apartment. As soon as I found out I was pregnant, before Junior disappeared, he had me stop working. Then he never came back home. I had no means of supporting myself. Then I tried to hurt myself. And now here I am."

"What does Ms. Daisha say? I mean, I can ask my parents if you could stay with us until you get on your feet. As a matter of fact, I wanted to talk with you about what's going on with me, too."

Mia looked at me, alarmed. "Are you okay? Did something happen?"

"Well, yes. But it's nothing bad. Ms. Daisha told me they're releasing me in about two weeks."

"Two weeks? Ms. Daisha spoke with me earlier, too. She also told me that I was going to be released in about two weeks also. She's looking for a family who can sponsor me, until I can get some work."

"My mom will be here early in the morning. I'll talk with her and let you know."

"You're the best. Thank you so much for trying to help me, Natasha. I've never had any real friends, I mean, except Junior."

"I'll do my best, Mia."

"Hey, Natasha, I'm sorry to bring your cousin up. And I know you haven't seen him in a long time. But what would you do if you ever saw him again?"

"What kind of question is that, Mia?" I snapped. "First of all, I'm never going to see him again, not if I can help it. I'll never forgive him, either, for ruining my life. Like I told you before, I prayed that he'd disappear forever."

"Do you mean that you prayed he'd die?" Mia asked.

"Um... Well..." I couldn't get the words out. "I didn't say die. I just said disappear. You know what, Mia? I really don't want to talk about this or him anymore. Okay?"

"Okay. I'm sorry."

I caught myself being impatient and immediately felt remorseful for taking it out on her. "No, I'm sorry, Mia. I didn't mean to snap at you like that. I want you to be able to ask me anything."

Mia grinned. "You know, Natasha, you're a very special young lady. You're so mature for you age. And believe it or not, you've helped me more than you know."

"Aww, Mia, you've helped me, too."

The phone rang at that very moment. It was Mom.

"Sweetheart, we'll be picking you up early tomorrow morning. Detective Fitz is going to have the lineup."

I panicked. "That's tomorrow?"

"Yes," Mom said. "Why? Are you not ready?"

"I'm ready, Mom. I just want to get it over with."

"Okay, my Love. Dad and I will see you in the morning."

"Okay, Mom. I love you."

"I love you, too, Honey."

I hung the phone up.

"What's going on?" Mia asked.

"Tomorrow I have to go see a police lineup of suspects in my case."

"You must be nervous."

"I am," I admitted. "But I have to do it. I'll be okay."

That night after I prayed, my mind wouldn't stop. I'd wished Mia didn't bring up Joe. But I didn't blame her. I chose to share my secret with her. It's only natural for her curiosity. But it had opened up a can of memories of him and the pain he inflicted on me. It made me wonder where he'd gone and if he'd ever come back. I couldn't bear to ever face him again. I had nothing but pure hate in my heart for him. I felt so much progress, yet that memory from my traumatic past was a thorn in my side. I prayed to God… If only He could erase my past memories.

## CHAPTER EIGHTEEN

# Lost Girl

Luke 15:3–6

Then Jesus told them this parable: "Suppose one of you has a hundred sheep and loses one of them. Doesn't he leave the ninety-nine in the open country and go after the lost sheep until he finds it? And when he finds it, he joyfully puts it on his shoulders and goes home. Then he calls his friends and neighbors together and says, 'Rejoice with me; I have found my lost sheep.'

I stepped out into the real world. It seemed like a foreign land to me. I had become accustomed to my small, safe world at the rehabilitation center. When we pulled up to the precinct, there were a swarm of NYPD cars all over. I held Mom and Dad's hands really tightly. My palms were clammy and sweaty.

"You're gonna do great, Sweetheart. We are here with you," Dad assured me.

"I know," I said, looking at him.

I swallowed hard, heart racing. I trembled while walking. My nerves were rattled. I looked all around me to make sure I didn't see anyone I knew. I was a little paranoid, thinking my attackers might be lurking. As we walked into the precinct, I quickly looked behind me to make sure we weren't being followed. I became suspicious.

"Tasha, it's okay," Mom said to me. "Don't be scared."

I nodded to indicate that I was fine.

Dad approached the front desk to ask for Detective Fitz. He greeted us shortly after.

"Good morning, Mr. and Mrs. McCarthy. Hi, Natasha."

I just smiled nervously.

"We'll make this as quick and painless as possible," the detective promised.

"Okay," I said under my breath.

"Now, Natasha, you don't have to worry. We are going into that room over there. They can't see you. The glass is a one-way mirror. The suspects will each have a number on their chests. I want you to relax and take your time. Look at each one carefully and let me know if you recognize any of them."

"Okay," I said stoically.

We walked into the room; the lighting inside was very dim. Mom and Dad stood right next to me. We were looking into another room with a white background. I felt a bit nauseated. I didn't know what to expect. All of a sudden, a bunch of young women started to enter the room. There were six of them, to be exact. I immediately looked over at Detective Fitz.

I whispered, "Is it all girls?"

"Yes. Just relax. Look at each one. Tell me if any of them looks familiar to you," he explained.

As all of them slowly walked in, I noticed that they all kind of resembled each other. One walked in, then the second girl, then the third, the fourth, and the fifth one walked in.

"There!" I yelped. "Oh, my goodness! That's Lucinda! Number five," I said excitedly.The sixth girl finally walked in. They all faced me.

"Are you sure?" Detective Fitz asked.

"I'm a hundred percent positive. That's Lucinda. She's the one I met at the hospital," I said, breathing hard.

"Okay. Great job, Natasha." He called number five to step forward. So she did. "Take one more good look. We need to be sure."

"Yes. That's her." I said, composed.

"Okay. I told you it's going to be painless."

"What now?" Mom asked.

"Well, we have more than probable cause to hold her now that Natasha has positively identified her. We will hold her for questioning. You don't have to stay. We'll give you a call and let you know what's next," Detective Fitz explained.

"Please let us know as soon as you find out anything," Dad said.

"I sure will. I gave you my word before, and my word still stands," he said as he shook Dad's hand.

"Thank you so much, Detective." Mom shook his hand, too.

In the car ride back to the center, I didn't know how to ask Mom and Dad if Mia could stay with us. But I just dove right in.

"Mom...Dad... I need to ask you both something."

Dad looked at me through the rearview mirror. "Sure, Sweetheart. By the way, you did great today."

"Thank you, Daddy. Um, do you know my friend Mia?"

"Do you mean the girl who's pregnant?" Mom asked.

"Yes, the pregnant girl."

"What about her?" Dad asked.

"Ah, well. She's basically homeless and is being discharged right around the same time as me."

"Okay…?" Dad looked calm.

"Well, I know this is a lot to ask. But I thought maybe she can stay with us until she gets on her feet?" I said, kind of cringing. I worried about how they would react to my very audacious request.

"Oh wow, Honey, we don't know anything about this girl and—" Mom said but I interrupted.

"But, Mom, *I* know her. She's a really nice person. She doesn't have a family. Her parents gave her up when she was a baby. Mia is a lost girl. I feel like I've known her my whole life. And I don't want to put you on the spot, but what would Jesus have us do? Did Jesus himself not talk about the one lost sheep? How He went out to save that one?"

My parents were thrown by my rhetorical questions.

"I'm sorry she didn't have a good life. How far along is she in her pregnancy?" Mom asked.

"She's five months along."

Mom continued. "What kind of job do you suppose she'll be able to get now? She's going to have her baby in just a few months."

"I don't know, Mom. I just think I met her for a reason. You and Dad always said that we can always make the world a better place, not just by saying things that make a difference, but by actually acting on making a difference. Right?" I pleaded.

"Honey, you're right," Dad chimed in. "I'll tell you what, how about you, Mom, and I talk with your friend Mia. We'd like to get to know her a little better. I might consider it. I do believe as Christians or just for the sake of humanity, sometimes, we are given challenging tasks to take on. Maybe this is one of them."

Mom just looked at him, stunned. "Phillip, are you sure about this?"

"Yes, the worst that could happen is that, things don't work out and we can still help her find a place of her own," he replied.

"Thank you, Daddy." I curled up behind him by the seat to hug him. "She's going to be so happy."

"Well, I said we should talk with her first. We have to be sure she's okay with it, too. And we are going to set rules," Dad said. "And you'll be back in school. I don't want this to interfere with your schoolwork."

"I know, Daddy. It won't. Thank you!"

We got back to the center in time for me to attend the afternoon group session. I couldn't wait to break the news to Mia. Mom and Dad planned on coming back the next day to talk with her. And if all went well, they planned on making the arrangements with Ms. Daisha. I felt like I was gaining an older sister, for a little while at least.

## CHAPTER NINETEEN

# The Truth Hurts

Luke 8:17

For there is nothing hidden that will not be disclosed, and nothing concealed that will not be known or brought out into the open.

A couple of months before I was admitted into the center, the trees were dressed with colorful warm leaves. Then the day of my discharge finally arrived. When we walked out, the trees were naked, the wintery air was cool, and silvery clouds surrounded the vibrant sun. Ms. Daisha made arrangements with my parents, who agreed to sponsor Mia and allow her to stay with us until she gave birth to her baby boy. Hopefully by then, Ms. Daisha would have helped to find Mia housing for low-income families. Mia had been so grateful. I'll admit, I was pretty happy, too. Auntie Lucy planned a welcome-home dinner at her house for me. I had to play it cool. After all, her house would bring back a flood of terrible memories to me. I hadn't been particularly excited about having the dinner there, but I didn't want to hurt my auntie's feelings. It just gave me great comfort that Joe no longer lived there anyway.

We went home first to get myself and Mia settled in. I had mixed feelings about being back at home. I loved being back with my parents, but I missed all of the girls I bonded with at the center, and Ms. Daisha, too.

As we approached the front door of Auntie Lucy's house, I felt this numbness. I had all kinds of emotions rushing through me. The same emotions I felt every time we spent holidays or birthdays there. Both occasions were supposed to be happy. But for me, they were feelings of nothing but grief. Auntie Lucy greeted us.

"Oh, Natasha!" she cried loudly as she hugged me. "Welcome back home! We've missed you so much."

I smiled. "Me too, Auntie Lucy."

She kissed Mom and hugged Dad. She looked over at Mia. "And you must be Mia. It's nice to finally meet you."

Mia smiled. "Thank you. It's nice to meet you, too."

"You can call me Lucy, Sweetheart," Auntie said.

The delicious smell of the food was everywhere. If I didn't know any better, it had been just like our Thanksgiving gatherings every year growing up. Auntie Lucy loved cooking. For dinner, she actually cooked a twenty-pound turkey. This turkey wasn't your usual. Auntie had a gift of making the juiciest, yummiest turkey. The gravy was also something out of this world. The table already had all of the fixings placed on it. There were collard greens, corn on the cob, rice with beans, homemade stuffing, caramelized sweet potatoes with marshmallows, and homemade garlic mashed potatoes. What a sumptuous sight.

"Wow! You did all of this for me?" I asked.

"Yes, Sweetheart," Auntie Lucy replied. "Today is a very special day. And I want you to know we all love you very much."

My tears welled up. I didn't know what to say. But my heart became full at that very moment. "Thank you. I love you all, too," I said, wiping my tears away.

It was great to see my cousin Lisa, too. I hadn't been the greatest example to my younger cousin. I just felt terrible that I had distanced myself from her only because she was Joe's little sister. She became collateral damage, unfortunately.

It felt like old times, just like when we were little. We talked and laughed. Mia fit in, too. It was as if we'd all known each other all of our lives. It was too good to be true, but we were actually having a great time. For the first time in a very long time, at that moment of laughter and love, I felt some kind of normalcy. That was all I ever wanted. Later on, there was a hard knock on the door.

"Lucy, were you expecting anyone else?" Mom asked.

"No, I wasn't," Auntie Lucy said while walking toward the door. She looked through the window of the door. "It's a gentleman. He looks kind of like a cop."

Dad looked surprised. "A detective?"

Auntie Lucy opened the door. "Hello, can I help you?"

"Hi, I'm Detective Fitz. Are—?"

Mom rushed to the door as soon as she heard the familiar voice. "Detective Fitz?"

"Mrs. McCarthy?" Detective Fitz looked confused.

"Is everything okay?" Mom asked. "How did you know my sister lived here?"

"I didn't," he said.

Mom looked confused.

"Come on in, Detective," Auntie Lucy said.

Mom introduced them. "Detective, this is my sister Lucy Murphy."

"Nice to meet you, Mrs. Murphy," he said.

"You can call me Lucy. Please have a seat."

They sat in the living room.

"What brings you here, Detective?"

Detective Fitz's face looked perplexed. "I don't know where to start. But I wanted to know, who else lives here with you, Lucy?"

"Ah, it's just me and my daughter Lisa. My husband and I have been separated for a few months.

Joseph. He's been staying with family out in Jersey," Auntie explained.

"Are you sure no one else lives here?" he asked.

"Ah, well…my son used to live with us. But he's been gone for almost six years."

"Do you know where he lives?" Detective Fitz asked.

Auntie looked down like she was embarrassed. "I'm so ashamed to say. But I haven't talked to my son since he left the military. He had been dishonorably discharged shortly after and never kept in touch with us. It's complicated, Detective. We've been estranged. I did my best to raise him to be a man of integrity and good character, but…" She broke down crying. Mom grabbed a hold of her.

Dad became upset. "Detective Fitz, what is this all about? I don't understand?"

"I'm sorry to hear that. There's a man involved in our investigation in Natasha's case, who used this address as his residence, based on our findings. We need to know if you know this man."

"What!?" Mom and Dad said simultaneously.

"We have a witness in custody who gave us information about him," the detective said.

"I don't understand. Who is this man?" Auntie asked, worried.

I stood by there in the living room, watching and listening to the whole thing. Droplets of sweat crept out from my hairline. I became a little nervous. Mia sat on the sofa, looking confused, too.

"Mrs. Murphy…Lucy, I want to show you a photo and you tell me if you know this man." Detective Fitz reached down into his folder. He pulled out what looked like a photo and showed it to her.

Auntie reached to grab the photo. "Oh, my word. Joe! That's my son!"

"Joe?" Mom stood beside her as she looked at the photo, as well. Shock was written all over her face.

"Oh, my goodness. Where is he? Is he arrested? I want to go see him. Lord knows I've been praying for me to find him," Auntie rambled.

"Mrs. McCarthy, can you come sit here with your sister?" Detective Fitz asked Mom.

Mom looked as if she didn't understand. She walked over and sat down with Auntie right by where Mia had been sitting, too.

"I am sorry to inform you, this man, who you identify as your son, is deceased," the detective said.

"No! No! No! No! Not my Joe!" Auntie sobbed with deep grief as Mom held on to her. She dropped the photo down on the coffee table.I noticed Mia taking a gander at it. Suddenly she screamed hysterically, "No! It's Junior! No! Why!?"

I ran over to look at the photo, as well. I couldn't believe what had been happening. I didn't recognize him. And I was in shock, too. "Mia, this isn't your Junior. It can't be."

"It's Junior, he's dead," she sobbed.

My head spun. I got so dizzy and faint. Darkness quickly came upon me.

The clouds were thick and dark. They transformed into the monster

I met so long ago. It hovered over that room of terror. What had I been doing lying on that dreary bed in the seedy motel room again? It was the place where I had faced evil for weeks. I heard the familiar eerie, deep voice.

"What's her name?"

"Natasha. I did good right, Boss?'

"Where did you find this girl again?"

"She was one of the girls I found at the hospital."

"We gotta get outta here."

I remembered this conversation in a dream. I took a good look at who had been asking the questions. It was the monster. He looked at me and I looked at him. *It can't be*, I thought at that very second. *I must be hallucinating.*

The heated conversation continued.

She said, "I'm sorry. You said to find girls that looked like her. You said—"

"I know what I said!" he yelled. "I told you to bring me pictures first! Didn't I?"

"Ahh…"

"Didn't I!?" he shouted again.

"Yes, you did. I'm sorry. I just figured she was exactly what you were looking for," she explained.

"We need to get out of here. Now!"

"Wait, what about Natasha?"

"We leave her behind."

"But…"

"But nothing! Let's get out of here now!" he shouted.

"Who is she?" she asked.

"We leave this one alone. She's been through enough already."

"What are you gonna tell Kage? You know you're throwing away money by leaving her behind?"

"Hey! I'm the boss here. Not you! Got it?" he yelled as he smacked her.

Then the monster walked over to me in a panic. We locked eyes. The dark, thick cloud; the monster began transforming himself into a man. The man was Joe. Joe was in that dreadful room with me. How could that be? He inserted a needle into my arm again.

There I fell into the dark abyss again.

I awoke in that room, tied up to the bed and everyone was gone.

"Natasha, Baby! Wake up!" Dad cried out with a cold towel on my head. "Baby, it's me, Dad. Are you okay?"

All I continued to hear were cries of anguish. Auntie was crying. Mom was crying. Mia was inconsolable. My mind grappled over this. I couldn't wrap my head around what had been happening.

"Mrs. Murphy, I need you to come down to the morgue to identify the body," Detective Fitz said.

"I need to call my husband Joseph. I want him to come with us, too," Auntie Lucy cried.

"Yes, of course," the detective agreed.

We were all sharing the same nightmare.

## CHAPTER TWENTY

# DEPARTED

ECCLESIASTES 9:5–6

> For the living know that they will die, but the dead know nothing; they have no further reward,and even their name is forgotten. Their love, their hatred, and their jealousy have long since vanished; never again will they have a part in anything that happens under the sun.

The atmosphere was heavy with grief and hollow hearts. We all decided to go in one car. Dad drove Auntie Lucy and Uncle Joseph's black Land Rover SUV to the morgue. Uncle Joseph was also in the car with us. As soon as Auntie broke the news to him, he came right over. Dad drove behind Detective Fitz's car. Mom sat in the front with Dad. Lisa, Mia, and I sat in the back. Mia and Auntie were inconsolable. Uncle Joseph held on to Auntie, trying to comfort her. Mom continued to weep, too. Dad kept it all together. I sat there with no expression on my face at all. I was in utter shock. Feelings of guilt also weighed on me.

I had prayed so many years for him to disappear forever. I didn't know what to feel or think at the time. I felt desensitized.

Soon after arriving at the morgue, Auntie just continued to whimper. The sounds of her cries were painful to listen to. I felt a lump in my throat.

The moment had arrived when we all stood outside of the room where Joe's body laid.

"Are you sure you are ready to go in?" Detective Fitz asked Auntie.

"Yes. I need to see my baby." She cried as Uncle Joseph embraced her. Uncle Joseph's eyes were red.

I needed to see him with my own eyes. I still couldn't believe it. I thought maybe it could be mistaken identity.

Mom asked that Mia, Lisa, and I to wait outside. But the three of us insisted to go in, as well. Mia became hysterical, crying again.

As Detective Fitz opened the door, Auntie and my uncle followed him and the rest of us followed behind them. The room was dove grey. There was a distinct smell in the room. There in the viewing room was what looked like a narrow table with a covered body. I stood behind with Lisa toward the back of the room. Lisa appeared too scared to stand close. The medical assistant stood next to Detective Fitz as she pulled the sheet off slowly. Auntie Lucy screamed loudly and fell over on top of Joe's body.

"My baby… I'm so sorry, my Love… No…" Auntie sobbed as she ran her fingers through his hair. She touched his face, then rubbed his forehead. She noticed the hole on the side of his head.Uncle Joseph stood by and looked shocked.

Mia ran up next to them and screamed, too. "Junior, what am I going to do without you?"

She almost fainted. Dad grabbed a hold of her and walked her outside of the room. I mustered up the courage to slowly walk up to where Joe's body was. I soon became nauseous and dizzy. As I stood there, my mind wandered off into the garden again.

The garden had been consumed with a thick fog. I walked slowly through it. I could hear the monster's voice talking.

I didn't understand what he was trying to tell me.

Then I heard, "Natasha, release him from his debt."

I didn't understand. "Release him from his debt?"

"Natasha, forgive him and free yourself," He said again."No. I can't forgive him. I won't forgive him. I will never forgive him," I insisted. The thick fog turned into a black cloud. The garden was no more. It was dry and empty. Straightaway, I heard a bizarre noise that came from the monster. It was a disturbing and painful wail. I got a glimpse of him down on the ground, hopeless and sad.

"Why do you cry, when you are the one who caused me so much pain?" I asked coldly. But the monster didn't stop crying.

"Your cries are empty to me. Am I to feel sorry for you now? I pray for God to judge you according to all of the anguish you caused me," I said and walked away.

"Tasha… Tasha…" Mom kept tapping me on my shoulder. "Honey, we have to go."

Auntie Lucy and the rest of us exited the room where Joe's body lay. It had been surreal. On the ride back home, Mia and I sat all the way in the back. Mia whimpered softly on my shoulder. Everyone in the car remained silent.

By the time we arrived back at Auntie's house, they seemed cried out. Once inside, I could hear the adults talking in the kitchen. Phone calls were being made. Lisa was so upset; she had excused herself. She needed time alone. Mia and I were the only two left sitting in the living room.

Then Mia whispered to me in despair, "Natasha, please don't tell me that Junior was the cousin you told me about? The one you told me who hurt you?"

I stood silently as I looked right into her eyes. Tears welled up and slowly rolled down my cheeks.

"Oh no," Mia said.

We both began crying as she leaned toward me to hug me.

"I'm so sorry," Mia said.

"He was a monster," I said softly.

"I guess I shouldn't really be surprised."

"Shouldn't be surprised about what?" I asked, confused.

"When Joe found me, he'd taken me to go live with him. I had just turned eighteen around then. At that time, I was still living with my foster parents. But I was miserable there. I was just a paycheck for them."

"So what are you saying?" I interrupted.

"My foster parents reported me missing because I just never came back home. The first night I left with him, I always suspected he might've spiked my drinks with something."

"What makes you think that?"

"Well, I don't think. I know. Because I don't remember most of that night and I only had two drinks with him. And the following morning after just meeting him, I woke up in the same bed with him. At first, it made me scared, but he promised to provide a better life for me. I thought my life was meaningless anyway, so why not just give in to his proposition?" Mia explained. "What choice did I really have?"

"Oh, my goodness. Mia, you were his victim?" I said, stunned.

"I guess I never really saw it that way. He favored me the most out of all of the girls."

"Girls? What other girls?"

"There were other girls. I think even younger than me at that time. He just explained that they worked for him. Although, he'd have me and the others take turns some nights, as to who would spend alone time with him," Mia said casually.

"What!? I can't believe it!"

"That went on for a while, but then I got pregnant and he changed. He told me that he loved me, and only me. I also grew to love him, over time."

"So he wasn't your boyfriend?"

"It kept me sane to call him my boyfriend. I felt a sense of stability believing that. But I know that Junior, deep down inside, loved me. I have to believe that because I'm carrying his baby."

Auntie Lucy walked in right at the time she said those last three words, "carrying his baby."

Auntie sat down next to Mia. She looked worried. "Mia, Sweetheart, tell me, what was your relationship with my son?"

"Mrs. Murphy, he was my boyfriend and we lived together," Mia said.

"And the baby is my…?"

"Yes, my baby is your grandson." Mia looked right into Auntie's eyes.

Auntie wept. "You're carrying my grandson?" Her voice quivered as she grabbed Mia closer to her and embraced her. "My Joe's legacy lives on. Oh, Sweetheart. This is a gift."

I cringed when I heard her say that. I'd grown to love Mia and her baby while in the center. But after knowing she was carrying Joe's baby, I didn't really know how to feel about it.

Detective Fitz informed my family earlier that he'd be in touch within the week with more information regarding a court date for the preliminary hearing. He didn't get into more details with Auntie that night because of the difficult news she had just received.

I needed to keep my secret concealed from the rest of my family. I had no idea what Detective Fitz uncovered in his investigation. But I had to trust where God was leading me to.

## CHAPTER TWENTY-ONE

# Freed Butterflies

John 8:32

Then you will know the truth, and the truth will set you free.

MANHATTAN, NEW YORK
TUESDAY, FEBRUARY 3, 1987, 9:00 a.m. SESSION

> "This is the time and place set for this preliminary examination in the case of the People of the state of New York versus Mr. Colin Lee Richards; case number H249721. The defendant is present. Would counsels please state your names and appearances for the record, please?"

This day had been distressful. As the counselors introduced themselves and the court addressed all to proceed, I noticed there were ten girls sitting in the courtroom, all of them holding each other's hands. I wondered who they were. When they first walked into the courtroom and sat down, I saw all of their heads bowed as they whispered under their breaths. It looked like they had been praying.

"Call your first witness," the court stated.

"Lucinda Watts, the witness herein, called by and on behalf of the People, was duly sworn and testifies as follows."

"Please step over here, Miss, and raise your right hand. You do solemnly swear that the testimony you are to give before this court to be the truth, the whole truth, and nothing but the truth so help you God?"

"Yes."

"Please take the stand and be seated. State your full name and spell your last name, please," the court clerk said.

"Lucinda Watts. W-A-T-T-S."

Lucinda had already been on the stand for about fifteen minutes. Clearly, she had been shaken up. The judge stopped the proceedings once to get her a tissue. All eyes were on her in the courtroom. Mia and I sat together with our hands clutched tightly. Then yet another question was asked and she answered.

"Well, yes, I was scared."

"If you were scared, why didn't you try to escape, or call the police?"

Lucinda began crying. "Well, because not only had they taken me, but they had my little sister, too. She's only fifteen. They threatened if I ever went to the cops or didn't do what they said, they would kill her and kill me, too." She continued to explain. "My job was to recruit new girls. They were making a lot of money. I just did what they told me to do."

"Who told you what to do?" the counselor asked.

"Kage and Junior."

"When you say Kage, are you referring to the defendant, Mr. Colin Lee Richards?"

"Yes. Everyone called him Kage. I never knew that his real name was Colin."

"And who is Junior?" the counselor asked.

"Junior was the big boss. He gave all of the orders."

"Okay, go on."

"The night I convinced Natasha to come with me, she thought I was a patient at the hospital, too. But I was only there to find more girls for them. Natasha was perfect. Junior was picky as to what kind of girls he wanted."

"What did he do with the girls?"

"Kage would drug them to the point where they just went along with what they wanted. Each girl was sold to different johns. You know, customers."

The questioning began getting more intense. Lucinda proceeded to answer the next question.

"Yes. Kage and Junior never allowed any girl to be let go, ever. The morning we left Natasha behind had been the first time Junior saw her. She was the new girl at that time. We just reported back to him every day with the money and amount of customers she serviced. But Junior tended to stop in on jobs. So that day, when he first saw Natasha, he freaked out. He said he knew her and wanted to let her go. I didn't understand why at first. And when I questioned Junior about it, he hit me. So we left her, and when Kage found out about it he was livid. Kage said that Junior messed up because she's a witness and all could go wrong. He worried their business could be ruined."

"What happened after that?" the counselor asked.

"A few weeks after that, things got really bad between Junior and Kage. They started screaming at each other. Kage insisted that we find Natasha and bring her back. Kage wanted to get rid of her."

"When you say get rid of her, what do you mean by that?"

"I mean, Kage wanted her dead. He considered her a liability. Junior wasn't having it. He told Kage that he hurt Natasha when she was little."

"Did he say how he'd hurt her?" the counselor asked.

"Yes. Junior said he sexually abused Natasha."

Loud gasps sounded in the courtroom. I couldn't believe what I had just heard. Mom and Dad's face turned white. It was as if they'd seen a ghost.

Auntie Lucy yelled, "Liar! How dare you lie about my son? He's not even here to defend himself."

"Order in this court!" the judge said as he beat the gavel against his bench. "Ma'am, one more outburst from you and I will have you removed from my courtroom."

Mom started to cry softly while Dad held her.

"Proceed," the judge ordered.

"You may continue, Ms. Watts," the counselor stated.

"Junior said that he abused Natasha for years. He didn't want any more pain inflicted on her. Kage got really angry. That's when all of a sudden, Kage pulled out his gun and shot him right in the head." Lucinda broke down sobbing.

There was another outburst in the courtroom.

"Lucinda, I'm here for you, Honey!" a woman yelled as she ran toward Lucinda.

"Oh, Mom." Lucinda cried as she hugged her mother.

Next to them stood a young girl who resembled Lucinda, it was her fifteen-year-old sister.

"Order!" the judge said.

Then the ten girls who were sitting toward the back of the courtroom, who were praying earlier, all walked over to Lucinda, and they hugged each other as a group. The ten girls began praying out loud, "The

Lord is my shepherd…" They continued praying on. "Yea though I walk through the valley of the shadow of death, I will fear no evil."

Everyone had been amazed, including the judge himself. Kage had an evil grin on his face. While the girls hugged Lucinda, a few of them began talking to her.

"We forgive you."

Another said, "It's not your fault."

Then another girl said, "We are all the same. We are sisters.

"Yes, we are here for you," another girl said.

Lucinda just sobbed.

At that very second, my head grew heavy. My eyes became blurred. I felt really lightheaded. Wooziness overcame me. I stepped into the breathtaking garden. It had been the same one where I had heard God's voice. Over by a beautiful, pink-blossomed tree, I saw thirteen cocoons. Little by little and one by one, each cocoon started to break open. The shells were slowly falling off each majestic, colorful butterfly. Each butterfly had its own unique blend of colors. I was in awe. I watched each one break free. But I noticed that out of the thirteen cocoons, only twelve of them broke free. I'd never seen anything like this, but the twelve butterflies just hovered over the one that hadn't yet opened. Then I saw the monster bent down, weeping. He wailed, and whimpered. His tears became a small stream along the ground where the beautiful flowers stood. I could hear him mumbling. I couldn't make out what he was saying. His words were muffled. The twelve butterflies then surrounded the monster. I didn't understand what was happening. The sun brightened up even more. The clouds were like beautiful decorations in the sky. I looked over ahead of me and could see several bright yellow sunflowers. They were everywhere. The light shined on the monster from the sky.

"God, what do you want from me?" I wept and I wept. "I can't forgive him. He hurt me really bad."

Right at that moment, the twelve butterflies hovered over me. The last cocoon stood all alone. Slowly each of the butterflies began changing into the girls. I gasped. I realized who they were. They were the ten girls from the courtroom, the eleventh girl was Lucinda, and the twelfth girl was Mia.

They all looked so beautiful, so peaceful and happy.

"What does this mean?" I asked.

"Those girls share the same monster as you," He said.

"They are Joe's victims, too?" I asked.

"Yes."

"Who is the girl in the last cocoon?"

"Natasha, the other butterfly is yet to be freed. The other butterfly is you," God's voice said.

"What?" I asked, still confused.

"Natasha, you have to forgive."

I cried loudly. I could still hear the monster's cries. I slowly walked over to it. Fear completely left my mind and spirit. I placed my hand on the monster's head.

"I forgive you. Joe, I forgive you."

I felt the heavy burden lift up out of my soul. Then steadily, the monster changed into a man. The man was Joe. His weeping stopped. I could hear a loud, crackling noise. It was the last cocoon. It started to break open. Swiftly, the butterfly swooped out of its shell. The butterfly had every single color of the rainbow on its wings. The colors looked just like the bed of roses I had seen in the garden before.

"Natasha, your garden is flourishing. This is just the beginning. Remember, you are like the tree of life."

It was right at that very moment that I knew the truth. Truth is the key, not only to freedom, but to salvation. I had been freed from bondage; the bondage that the devil took pleasure in keeping me in. I learned that because of what God did for us by sending His Son Jesus Christ, our sins have been forgiven.

I had been saved by grace through my faith. My faith had been the only thing I refused to give up. And so, it was my responsibility to forgive the one who trespassed against me. This truth has forever set me free.

# Epilogue

Isaiah 61:2–3

> To proclaim the year of the Lord's favor and the day of vengeance of our God, to comfort all who mourn, and provide for those who grieve in Zion—to bestow on them a crown of beauty instead of ashes, the oil of joy instead of mourning, and a garment of praise instead of a spirit of despair. They will be called oaks of righteousness, a planting of the Lord for the display of his splendor.

Present day…

The beautiful city of Miami reflected relaxation, vacations, and fun in the sun. It was a breath of fresh air to be here and spread the message of hope. My team and I were here for only a few days to pitch another opening of an additional facility here. We already had our first building established in Manhattan, New York, and our second facility in Los Angeles, California. The three of us anxiously sat in the waiting room until they called us in.

My name was called. "Mrs. McCarthy-Morgan"

"Yes," I said as I stood up. "Hi, very nice to meet you, these are my partners, Ms. Lugo and Ms. Watts," I introduced them as I shook her hand.

"Good morning, Ladies. Very nice to meet you," the woman said. "Come on in."

We walked into an auditorium filled with hundreds of people. We'd never presented to a large audience like this before. The presenter began talking.

"Good morning, everyone, our guests have finally arrived here today from New York City. I am proud to introduce the founder and owners of the Tree of Life Rescue Foundation. It is a nonprofit organization for the rescue and healing of all sexual-abuse and human-trafficking victims. The Tree of Life Rescue Foundation was founded in 2005. These women of faith and courage have dedicated their lives to facilitate the rescue and healing of girls, boys, women and men by sex slavery in the human-trafficking industry. It is also for those who have been sexually abused as children. They facilitate a wonderful staff, which provide inspiration and guidance with love. They also facilitate empowerment classes, therapeutic services, and a sanctuary that help ease them into the healing process. There are also educational classes and training for the warning signs and red flags of the predators in this industry. Most importantly, their foundation was founded on the principles of God's love for us and the comfort that He also provides for all. Please welcome Mrs. Natasha McCarthy-Morgan and her wonderful team."

The crowd roared. It was like a dream watching all of these people who were giving us a standing ovation. It had been inevitable that the waterworks began; I discreetly wiped the tears from my eyes.

After we were done with our presentation, I felt a great sense of relief and accomplishment at the same time. The morning had been a successful one. It looked like we were getting the thumbs up for a new facility in Miami. The ladies and I were in the car on our way back to the hotel when I received a phone call. It was a FaceTime call.

I picked up the call and it began connecting. "Oh, it's Joel. Hey, Honey. Say hi. We're all in the car now."

"Hello… Hi, Mom… Hello Ms. Watts," he said.

All of the ladies simultaneously said hello as they waved and blew him kisses.

"I tried calling Mom first, but it went straight to voicemail."

"Hi, Honey. I'm sorry, Love. My phone died," Mia said.

"You look so handsome! Where are you going?" I asked him.

Joel had just turned twenty-one and recently graduated four years of college. "I have great news!"

"What is it?" I asked.

"The NYPD investigator called me! They are beginning the process to get into the police academy," he said excitedly.

"Aww, that's wonderful, Honey. I'm so proud of you," I said.

"Yes, Sweetheart," Mia chimed in. "I'm proud of you, Son."

"I can't wait to become a police officer, so I can make a difference, like you all are doing," he said.

"Aww, Joel, you're going to be a fine police officer."

"I hope to one day in the future be able to be a part of your company," he said with a wide smile.

"Oh, you will, Joel. Right now, the police department works very closely with us. You already have the heads up on certain protocols and procedures. I can't wait for one day for you to be a part of this. Hey, one day, you never know, we may pass the torch to you."

"Yes. Okay, Aunt Tasha and Mom. Oh, and you, too, Ms. Watts. I gotta run. I have to meet my investigator in two hours," Joel said.

"God bless you, Sweetheart," his mom said. "We love you."

I am so proud of this young man who ironically looked and was a twin of his father. I also became his Godmother. He has a heart of gold, and ever since he was a little boy, he always wanted to help people and always wanted to learn more about God's Word. He is indeed a gift to us all. His life reminds me that in all things, God works things out for good in the end. God turned our ashes into beauty. And, well, as for myself, I also had three beautiful children of my own with my other half, Andrew. My garden had grown and continues to flourish and bear fruit today.

THE END

# A Note from the Author

Dear Friends,

Thank you for taking the time to read *The Deflowered Garden* novella. I'm sure this story was a tough one to read, because as the author, it was certainly a tough one to write. God placed it in my heart to write about this particular affliction that, unfortunately, so many have been affected by—and still are being affected today.

Ever since I was a little girl, I had a fascination with flowers and nature itself. I loved to draw them, too. I love what gardens represent. They remind me of life, beauty, color, light, and uniqueness. All of the qualities made up in humanity. In the garden, it represents the love, peace, and abundance that God created and intended for all of us. But it is also the same beautiful place where sin crept in and made a home for itself. This book speaks of the evidence of how God takes what the enemy used to harm you, and turns it around for your good. In the Bible, in Romans 8:28, it says, "And we know that in all things God works for the good of those who love him, who have been called according to his purpose." It doesn't say "in some things," it doesn't say "in the good things"; it says in ALL things. Even in the bad things, God works it for the good. This could be a scripture that some may have a hard time wrapping their heads around. Questions may arise, like why do bad things happen to good people, let alone to a child? There are some things that we will never understand or truly have the answers to. God's ways are not our ways. The way He thinks is entirely different to the way we think. The truth is that evil entered the world because of sin through the garden, and fractured humanity. The good news is that God sent His only Son, Jesus Christ, to save the world from it.

We've all had bad things happen to us, whether in our relationships, to ourselves, in our families, in marriage, at work, or in school. What we decide to do with the experiences of those bad things in our lives is pivotal to where the direction of our lives go. We also need to realize that no matter what, forgiveness is always necessary for the completion of victory in our lives, as well. In *The Deflowered Garden*, Natasha had a terrible secret. The devil loves secrets. He uses our secrets to keep us in bondage. Those dark secrets keep us in the dark. They are not meant to be kept away in hiding. In the Bible, in John 12:46, Jesus said, "I have come into the world as a light, so that no one who believes in me should stay in darkness." This is a truth that we must embrace and believe. The devil tries to keep us locked away in our secrets of shame and condemnation. But I believe our transgressions are meant to be shared with others who may have suffered the same. When you believe that Jesus Christ died for us because God loves us that much, Jesus's light shines and overpowers that darkness in which we once lived. The chains of your secrets or past suddenly break free.

I want to remind you that your pains or problems are not a curse, but rather a blessing. They are gifts meant to inspire others—that because you've walked through the valley and made it out into the light, it's proof that God is good not just some of the time, but is good ALL the time.

I pray and encourage that you always find hope and believe you "can do all things through Christ who strengthens you" (Philippians 4:13). Amen!

With love in Christ,
Tanya South

If you or anyone you know needs help, please call the National Child Abuse Hotline at 1-800-422-4453 or the National Human Trafficking Hotline at 1-888-373-7888.

CPSIA information can be obtained
at www.ICGtesting.com
Printed in the USA
LVHW011153060319
609693LV00006B/35

9 780310 103554